THE BOOK OF WANDERERS

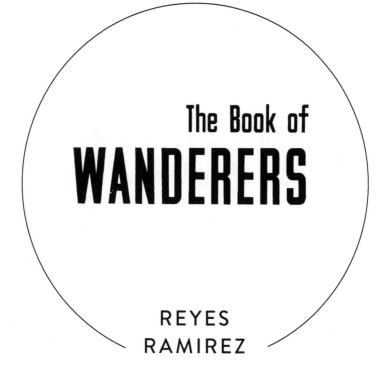

The Book of
WANDERERS

REYES
RAMIREZ

THE UNIVERSITY OF
ARIZONA PRESS
TUCSON

The University of Arizona Press
www.uapress.arizona.edu

We respectfully acknowledge the University of Arizona is on the land and territories of
Indigenous peoples. Today, Arizona is home to twenty-two federally recognized tribes,
with Tucson being home to the O'odham and the Yaqui. Committed to diversity and
inclusion, the University strives to build sustainable relationships with sovereign Native
Nations and Indigenous communities through education offerings, partnerships, and
community service.

ISBN-13: 978-0-8165-4327-4 (paperback)

Cover design by Leigh McDonald
Cover photo: *Clavadistas at La Quebrada, 1973*, photographer unknown
Designed and typeset by Leigh McDonald in Calluna 10/14 and Telmoss WF (display)

Publication of this book is made possible in part by the proceeds of a permanent endowment created with the assistance of a Challenge Grant from the National Endowment for
the Humanities, a federal agency.

Library of Congress Cataloging-in-Publication Data are available at the Library of Congress.

Printed in the United States of America
♾ This paper meets the requirements of ANSI/NISO Z39.48-1992 (Permanence of Paper).

For my mom, my sister, my niece, my nephew, my love

without whom I'd still be lost

We were not alone
when we created children
and looked into their eyes
and searched for perfection

. . . .

How could we be alone
We searched together
We were seekers
We are searchers
and will continue
to search
because our eyes
still have
the passion of prophecy.

—FROM TOMÁS RIVERA'S
"THE SEARCHERS"

CONTENTS

FOREWORD

IN THE OPENING STORY, Iturbide Villalobos II, aka "The Marvel," one of the greatest luchadores of his time, shares the wisdom of showmanship with his son: "A wrestler is a liar in that he tells stories with his body. . . . I lie to be honest about what I can't say or do otherwise." That statement will resonate with readers of these compelling stories as the settings wander away from realism and into the realm of the magical and the fantastic. Imagine a woman whose mole is a mesmerizing third eye. Imagine the colonization of Mars. And beware, the zombie apocalypse is nigh. No matter how far into the future or into the strange these narratives travel, their plotlines bring the reader closer to our present embattled climate, where class disparity, racial prejudice, and xenophobia continue to sicken our social and political health.

Reyes Ramirez is not a liar but a truth teller, offering us a blunt glimpse into the lives of undocumented immigrants whose fight for their rights in the early stories of the collection is echoed in the premise of "Ximena DeLuna v. The New Mars Territory." There, a laborer gives birth on Mars and sues the colony for her child to be allowed to enroll in the white-only school. Indeed, white supremacy is alive and well, even a planet away, but so too is the tireless activism of those who challenge it.

Connecting this gathering of poignant stories is the grief or absence felt by the protagonists, like Xitlali Zaragoza, the superhero curandera, who has a prayer and an herbal concoction to ward off everyone's otherworldly menaces but is unable to treat the heartbreak of her estrangement from her daughter.

And that zombie apocalypse we encounter later in the book? With the past fading from memory after years of contending with this cataclysmic threat, there is both an opportunity for survivors to reimagine and rebuild a broken society and a chance for a group of racists to resurrect old systems of oppression, their new settlements white ones, "as originally intended until history was routed in the wrong direction." The battle for the human soul rages on.

Reyes, an avowed Houstonian, makes a foundation of his beloved city and home state, where most of the collection is set, inspired by Texas's own complicated historical timeline. The lead character in "Lilia" gestures toward this bittersweetness: "To remember things in Houston is to become its enemy and its favorite child. I suppose that depends on the history you choose to remember." For Reyes, these histories are inextricable from one another, and thus must be negotiated simultaneously, the good side by side with the bad, hope chained to despair, dream nestled against nightmare. How more real and substantive can an experience be than that? Enter the wonder and horror of *The Book of Wanderers* and find out for yourself.

—*Rigoberto González*

THE BOOK OF
WANDERERS

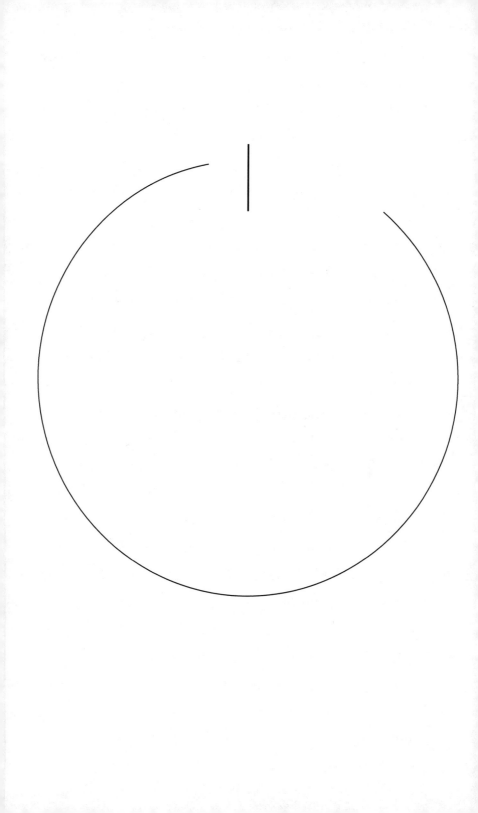

This theory obviously worked out somehow. Once the bell rang for his first official match with the now-defunct regional company Southwest Wrestling Association, Iturbide "The Marvel" Villalobos II, as we know him now, was born.

By that, I mean The Marvel established a sequence of maneuvers that ended his matches the same way thereafter. The Marvel fell onto his stomach and his opponent, the now-deceased John "The Butcher" Stallion, grabbed The Marvel's left arm, placed it between his thighs and locked his fingers around The Marvel's forehead. The crossface overextended The Marvel's neck backward while the scissor lock pulled The Marvel's left arm from its shoulder socket. The Marvel let out growls between his bared teeth. Someone clapped. Someone else whistled. Someone yelled, "Let's go Marvel!" The Marvel slammed his closed fist on the mat in intervals. The crowd chanted to his rhythm, "Mar-vel, Mar-vel, Mar-vel." Some stomped their feet. Some clapped.

Gaining strength from their encouragement, The Marvel pushed his entire torso up from the mat, brought his knees to his chest, and struggled to rise to his feet. The Butcher tried to keep his submission locked in. The Marvel grabbed The Butcher's trunks with his right arm for leverage and flexed his left arm. As he stood, The Marvel forced The Butcher's legs over each of his shoulders, setting him up for a powerbomb. The Butcher punched The Marvel's head as many times as he could to escape, but it was too late. The Butcher was slammed so hard onto the mat that sweat billowed from the wrestlers' slick bodies and vanished into light. The crowd roared.

The Marvel backed up into a corner and shook his fists in front of his chest until he took profound breaths that calmed him down. He met his hands as though in prayer, then stretched them out beyond his shoulders, each hand spread open. The Marvel then hunched and calmly waited for The Butcher to stand up. He did, dazed, then twirled around and faced The Marvel. The Marvel pounced on him, put The Butcher into a headlock, and used his right arm to place The Butcher's left arm against the back of his neck. Then The Marvel clutched The Butcher's trunks with his left arm and lifted him up into the air. The Marvel kept The Butcher there, having formed a single vertical line composed of two bodies radiating with stadium lights. The Marvel then leapt and fell back, his body parallel to the mat. He maintained The Butcher's body straight up and smashed his head down onto the mat like a missile into a sea. The crowd cringed as The Butcher's head bounced off the mat before his body collapsed like an old house. The Marvel covered him with a lateral press. Everyone, in a single voice, counted along, "1-2-3." The bell rang. Everyone cheered. It was the same order of events each time: a comeback, a powerbomb, charge up, a jumping vertical drop brainbuster, pin. Barely a year into his debut, The Marvel captured his first championship with the SWA, and it was only then that El Lobo finally applauded for his son.

This was around when my father turned twenty and dated my mother. She was a year older and completely enamored with him. She said he had the body and intelligence of a man with years of experience. "Ay, you should've seen him. Built like a bronzed god but as smart as someone who never stopped reading. But the ambition, mi amor, in his eyes and when he made love was really what sold him. I knew he would be great, and I knew I was great, too. We could be great together."

My question was, "Why do you stay married to him?"

My mother was a wrestler who went by Rosa, real name Rosario Araceli Itzel. She wore red latex wrestling shorts, a matching halter top that exposed her cleavage all bunched up, and red boots that laced up right underneath her knee. Her black hair flowed between her shoulder blades like a waterfall made up of the night sky. "They got me all dressed up like a puta," she said, "but I was the most dangerous puta on the planet."

Her favorite move sequence, and everyone else's, was her finisher, which went as follows: She put her opponent in a standing headlock, their skull compressed between her right forearm and bicep while their bent-over ass stuck out behind her. Rosa shot her left fist in the air and screamed. The crowd cheered. My mother then ran forward, her opponent clumsily paced along like a punished child. She jumped and crashed their face down onto the mat. Rosa then stepped over their body, back toward her opponent, and anchored her right foot between her opponent's thighs, crossed their left foot into the crease of their right knee and folded their right foot behind her right calf muscle. The resulting pressure of the folded right knee pinched down on their left ankle so that Rosa could use this as leverage to bend backward, her body arched over enough for my mother's hands to clasp around her opponent's neck, torso jutting up toward the ceiling. Her skin stuck to her ribcage as though wings attempted to break out into flight. Her opponent's legs were tangled in a knot, and their head bent back. My mother's black hair spilled over their face as though devouring them. Their arms flailed until they feebly slapped the mat in surrender.

She never made it as big as my father, though I consider her his equal in many ways. "Men don't like competition. Not real competition, anyways," Rosa said in a live promo that got her in trouble. Since she contractually couldn't work for another company, she served as The Marvel's valet to appease the SWA's management desire to punish her while still capitalizing on Rosa's fame. Her catchphrase became, "Tan fuerte," while she rubbed his abs. History is history.

And for such a strong woman, I wondered why my mother always let my father break her heart, over and over again, when he would cheat or go weeks without talking to her when he traveled abroad. "I don't know. Es lo que es," she answered, swirling a cocktail of gin and rose water in her hand. I asked my father once during a training session why he kept doing such awful things, handing my mother so much pain like that.

"In my line of work, boy, the body is a conduit of pain. Everything on it is susceptible to harm, and I am obliged to exploit it. Just how the butcher knows to cut two to four inches from the aitchbone of the pig to maximize the meat of the swine's rear leg, I know how to use the arm to inflict as much pain as possible. Consider the arm as a straight angle that when hyperextended beyond 180 degrees, pulls the arm from its socket and bends the elbow opposite of how God intended it to. A good butcher of the living body will also know that the converse is true, that forcing the arm to bend into an acute angle, to zero degrees if you will, does this, too. Perhaps Euclid never fully mapped the geometry of our bodies, but I've culled his work to my use. You may think such maneuvers are impractical in a real fight, but good art has never had to worry about being burdened with such babosadas as reality."

"You didn't answer my question," I said.

"What was it?"

"Why do you break her heart like that?"

"I do not understand the question. You cannot *break* a heart, mijo. But she's sensitive. She still loves me, and I still love her. No lo entenderías," he said before putting me in an armbar. I tapped out to submit, feeling the ball joint of my arm ripping out of my shoulder. But he wouldn't stop, so I began pounding the bottom of his feet with my fist, even attempting to bite his fat calf, which he simply smothered me with. When he let go, I cried on all fours as he smoothed his shorts.

"Why would you do that?" I asked.

"Another babosada. Why didn't you get out of it?"

"How can I get out of it if you wouldn't let me go?"

"How is that my problem? Puras estupideces today, mijo."

A typical answer from Iturbide II. Broken people go for other broken people, as though they can pull their ruins together and form something whole. That's what I like to think, anyways.

I don't know what I expected from him. He always gave answers like that, as far as I can remember. My mother said he didn't do that until after he won his first major championship, the one I saw on TV at the hospital while holding my dying grandfather's hand when I was eight years old. I hadn't seen my father in person up to that point, only on televised matches, as he had been traveling the world ever since I was born. I remember looking up at the screen, and The Marvel walking down the ramp to his entrance music, solemn and staring at the ring. He broke his glare to gift his wrist bands and T-shirt to children that screamed his name. The Marvel blessed them with his merchandise, kissed them on the forehead or shook their hands, and the commentators showered him with praise. I think my grandfather, El Lobo, could sense the anger welling up within me and asked me to get him something to drink. He never said water, by the way, even as the cirrhosis crumpled up his liver. I had to take my time in smuggling him a beer from an assistant he had on call from his wrestling academy, waiting for me in the parking lot.

"How's El Lobo holding up?" he asked. I shrugged and hid the beer in my backpack underneath my books. By the time I got back to my grandfather's room, The Marvel had already won the American Wrestling Enterprise World Heavyweight Championship. He stood on the turnbuckle and held the golden belt in the air while the crowd cheered. His father died alone. One of the first memories I have of my father, in fact, is him explaining that moment to me.

"The referee counted to three and that was it. He gave me the belt, and it was weightless. I climbed up to the second rope on the nearest turnbuckle and held it to the sky. When I looked out into the crowd, I could see nothing, the heavy lights blinding me with their pure whiteness, and no one had bodies anymore, including myself. Everyone was cheering so I could only hear the collective chants of my name vibrating the air around my body, and I breathed it into my lungs. When I exhaled, I think my soul clung onto the escaping air and traveled around that arena of what had to have been at least fifty thousand people shouting my name. I don't know how long that went on for, but it seemed like an eternity. That must have been how Adam and Eve felt before the primordial shame was brought upon them. I have been shown paradise and I want nothing less. Not for me and not for you, niño."

I think my question had been, "Did you ever think about me when you were gone?" It's sort of irrelevant now, but that's when he began training me to be a wrestler like him, like his father was. The Marvel would go on to be the longest serving world champion in AWE history. He inspired love from crowds all over the world every night he wrestled, and he returned home to teach me how he'd done it, putting me in submission holds and lecturing me.

"A wrestler is a liar in that he tells stories with his body. He only makes it seem he is hurting his opponent. I'm such a great liar because every one of my lies has a bit of me in them. You see, I don't lie to protect myself. I'm no coward. I lie to be honest about what I can't say or do otherwise. In fact, you could say my lies aren't lies at all. When I slam my opponent's head into the mat, I do it so that it does not actually harm him. But the desire for me to win at the expense of his defeat is honestly there, mijo. I lie this damn well because the crowd must believe me. The crowd is life. If they did not want me, then I would not be great. If they did not want me to be great, I'd be dead. Here I stand, my boy," Iturbide Villalobos II said.

He never realized that once you're recognized as a liar, no one will believe either your lies or truth. To be a good liar is to consistently tell stories, and I would go as far as to say that the truth gets in the way of a good story. My father never believed what he did was dishonest. That's why the greatest liar of all time is Iturbide "The Marvel" Villalobos II. That is my inheritance.

NI SABES, TOMÁS DE LA PAZ

DAY ONE

YOU HAD NEVER DONE a day's worth of real work in your fucking life, much less built anything that people could rest their two whole feet on. When you looked at your hands, you noticed how pale and clean they were. The skin on them "bronzeado," your friends joked. "Pull yourself a nice white girl." Your mom said the same thing but proudly.

Meanwhile, John, your white boss, loaded boxes upon splintery boxes of toys, fireworks, pool tables, pipes, etc. by the Houston Ship Channel at age thirteen when his father laughed at him because he didn't have money to buy a bike. "And man, was I the richest goddamn kid in sixth grade," John said.

But Rodrigo's hands were wonders: tanned from the sun, yet pasty, ashen from the scrapings of dead, smoldered skin and crumbs of sheetrock, wood chips and cement board; his palms were mapped with cracked scars, glistening blisters, and deep, dark pits filled in with hardened, black blood rimmed with purplish, greenish, yellowish bruises; his fingers were bulbous, bloated like a carcass in the sun at the knuckles but stringy, loose at the phalange and scaly, stocky, and rubbery as uncooked meat, mostly discolored, and chunky from corns, calluses, and years of work. You looked at your soft hands.

Rodrigo grinned and asked for your name when you two were first introduced by John.

"Tomás."

John hadn't bothered to mention it. "Tomás," Rodrigo repeated. "¿De dónde eres?" When a fellow Brown person asks where you're from, they don't really mean just you.

"Well, mi papa es de El Salvador," you said, which wasn't the whole truth since your dad wasn't around and your mom was from Mexico. But with half-truths came half the work.

"El Salvador. Me too," Rodrigo said with a grin.

You grinned too and started ripping boxes open. Or, tried to start ripping boxes but actually couldn't because the cardboard was not old and the last heavy thing you lifted was your little nephew asleep on the couch when he was four. "Tomás, hombre," Rodrigo tsked as he moved you aside and ripped the box just like that. You hated your smooth palms.

While the two of you worked in the sloppy heat, Rodrigo sang a sad song you thought sounded familiar.

"¿Lo sabes?"

"No."

"This song se va, 'Desde que la gente nació, y uno vió la otra, sonrió y le dijo, hola y te amo.'"

Since people were born, and one saw the other, he smiled and told her, hello and I love you. It had been one of the more beautiful things you heard up to that point in your life.

"It's a canción from El Salvador," he said. "It talks about la Guerra." You knew which guerra, as there's only one guerra every Salvadoran you met talked about.

"Ah," you said as you nodded.

"¿Has visitado El Salvador?" Rodrigo asked.

"No."

"Why?"

"I don't know," you shrugged. "I never had the chance."

"Pues," Rodrigo sighed, "you'd like. Todas las cipotas would jump on you."

"All the what?"

"Cipotas. ¿No sabes que significa cipota?" Rodrigo asks with a curl to his lip.

"No. Lo siento."

"Noooombre. Vamos a cambiar eso, bicho."

You were surprised to hear that but flattered.

"Why is that?" you asked.

"Se ponen aburridas." You weren't so flattered. Still, you asked Rodrigo many questions as you two constructed a perplexing table. *What's another word? Cachimbón. What's a drink you recommend from there? Regia. What's another word? Puchica, no recuerdo mas palabras ya, bicho.*

"Were you in the war?" you finally asked, which was a really dumb question.

"Fui un boy, pero sí. I could write libros about it." He motioned a large stack.

You worked until you were light-headed and never took a break because Rodrigo never took a break, not even to sip water. You were jealous, whiny jealous, that as the sweat stains of his shirt remained the same small size, you wanted to lie down and shiver, let the small film of moisture that lined the inside of your mouth pool somewhere along your cardboard tongue. But you didn't and even tried to stifle grunts with each push of node A into slot B of an entertainment center with Chinese instruction sheets. Rodrigo completed all this with such ease that his humming never stopped.

When he finished a poker table, he slapped his hands together and rubbed, looked into your eyes and asked, with a mountainous smile that revealed a golden incisor etched with something you couldn't see, "'Stás bien, primo?"

"Fasho," you said.

"Eh?"

"Que si," you clarified.

When it came to closing time, you waved to Rodrigo. He did not seem tired in the slightest bit, but happy. Rodrigo looked at the murky sun in the distance. You thought about saying goodbye to John but remembered that he paid you next to shit; also, you saw him serve himself a paper cup of tequila earlier. So fuck it, you thought.

When you got home later, you saw that your thighs resembled a hurt cat that shirked when you touched it. Your mother smirked at your limping, "¿Estás aprendiendo?"

"Hey, 'amá?" you called out to your mom.

"¿Sí?"

"Do you know what our lineage is, our ancestry?"

"Pues, mi mamá es mexicana con español, mi padre de gente indígena y something else porque his eyes were blue."

"¿Mi papá?"

"Híjole, mijo. I don't know. Probably indígena y something else como los otros. His skin, y tu también, is very light. Con europeo maybe. No sé, mijito."

"Qué bayunco . . ." you said, a word you heard before, though you weren't sure if you used it correctly.

"¿Qué dijiste?" your mom asked with a hand on her hip.

You showered, cupped warm water and poured it onto the redness of your thighs and breathed deeply. After, you researched and found that Salvadorans were originally Pipil and Lenca that could be mixed with Spanish, Dutch, French, Danish, Italian, Irish, Czech, Russian, Arab, Palestinian, Jewish, African, etc. That the Civil War raged for more than twelve years, the U.S. and Soviet Union having fed weapons and money to the government so that people like your father and Rodrigo either died or wandered the earth in exile.

When you slid into your bed to sleep, you wondered if Rodrigo had seen bodies just lying there.

DAY TWO

Your thighs were swollen, and your neck started to hurt while you slept, so you contemplated calling in sick but realized you'd feel like a little bitch. You kept John's number on speed dial during the thirty-minute drive there just in case.

You'd been a waiter at a sushi joint, a congressional intern, a writing tutor, some other prissy jobs, but never had you ever constructed a couch in the Houston heat, itchy sweat rolling down crevices you never noticed before. When you looked at Rodrigo, who wore a faded blue hat with the Enron logo, a white polo with all the buttons buttoned, bleached jeans, and bright sneakers that hadn't been cool since the '90s, he swept the floor with an efficient swoon, as though dancing.

You checked in with John, whose eyes were bulgy and red, and he pointed to a corner rife with crinkly boxes before tossing you a tube of wood glue. "Some of those shits might be a little broken," he said. And yes, some of them were. Composite wood dining room chairs not fit for the average American ass because widget A was too cracked to accept doohickey B. And when you came across such a dilemma, you called Rodrigo over. He tsked, adjusted his hat, and fixed it A-OK, "bien suavecito."

Rodrigo assembled a black futon frame with leftover screws from a poker table, covered up white scratches on a wooden bookcase with brown permanent marker, hammered rusty nails into the fractured corner of a box spring. John then sold them to mothers and newlywed couples with a grin. As Rodrigo placed his knee over the glued crack of a chair, he looked up at you and asked, "¿Has tenido sexo?"

"What?"

Rodrigo put down his tools, made a punching motion in the air with his fist, and whistled to mimic the act of coitus.

"Well, yes."

Rodrigo chuckled and nodded in approval. "Tú sabes que, when you finish sexo with una mujer, if you shake Coca-Cola, así," he shook his hand and simulated the fizzing by using his teeth pressed against his bottom lip, "you put it in her . . . tú sabes . . . después de que terminas y no baby." His hand, flat, sliced the air. You weren't shocked at the idea because the internet had shown you many things. You were shocked that you found someone who believed it. His eyes looked into yours and his face readied to be smug because you were supposed to tell him you hadn't thought of it, college boy. You started to laugh. Rodrigo probably believed it was a laugh of an epiphany and joined in.

"Do you have any children, Rodrigo?"

"No," he said.

"Did you ever want them?"

"No."

You then asked where the water was. Rodrigo shook his head with an emphatic "no." When you went to John, he informed you that the furniture store used to be an auto repair shop, that any sort of water dripped out of the musty bathroom sink. As you left his office where the bottle of tequila near his desk was nearly empty, John said, "I wouldn't drink out of that sink, thing's cursed." But I really don't have much of a choice, you thought as you swallowed what spit was left in your mouth.

You marched to the bathroom, whose sour smell was noticeable before you reached the door, but Rodrigo called out from a corner behind the mattresses, "Aquí, hombre." He held a jug in the familiar shape of an iced tea brand. Rodrigo took a swig and offered it to you. An I-know-something-you-don't-know smile grew across his face. You didn't know how to thank him and drank. It was a cheap beer but refreshing nonetheless. You drank it like a cure.

"Ah?" Rodrigo hummed.

"Ah," you responded.

And as the two of you sat in a room that must've been storage for disassembled engines, you pointed at the door with your thumb. Rodrigo tossed the notion away with a flick of his hand, "He's drunk. Very."

"Living the dream 'n shit, I guess."

"¿Cómo?"

"Never mind."

You two continued to swig warming beer in silence until Rodrigo raised a finger to his lips, hunched over to a cracked-in-half desk, struggled in opening a rusted drawer, and pulled out a stack of Polaroid pictures rubber banded together. He handed them over to you one by one after he looked at them and chuckled. Each picture was of a different woman, some in nice sundresses or tight jeans, some smiling, some laying on a couch, but none ever looked at the camera.

"What are these?"

"Womens."

"I can see that."

"Mujeres que yo . . . tú sabes . . ."

He made that punching motion in the air again.

"All of them?"

Rodrigo stuck his tongue out between his teeth and giggled, nodding up and down.

"Fuck, you gotta tell me your secret someday."

"Mira," he said as he handed over another Polaroid: a woman laid out on a bed. The camera must have been at the foot of the mattress as her black hair disappeared into the darkness of the room at the top of the picture. Her bottom half was under a white blanket that hugged her hips and legs, which made her seem like a mermaid; she wasn't looking at the camera either because she was asleep. What you remember most about the picture was the flash created a perverse aura on her torso, large, brown breasts illuminated as in some Goya painting.

"¿Una mexicana de Jalisco, eh?" he commented.

"Yeah, she's beautiful." Even though you were creeped out, you couldn't deny she was just that: beautiful. Her turned face was at some sort of peace, lips shut, cheek smooth, the other half of her face rested on the pillow. You wondered if that's the face everyone made during sleep after sex. Good sex, the exhausting kind that happens at the peak of a happy relationship, you imagined.

"Ay, how I loved her."

"What happened?"

"Pues, tú sabes. Vida."

"Sorry to hear that."

"Nah. Está bien. Womens, they come and they go."

"Fasho."

"Bueno . . . Let's go back to work. El jefe check sometimes."

You fashioned some more chairs, a couch, and a bed frame with missing slats. The two of you didn't talk, and the beer sweat collected in your shirts. When it came to closing time, you weren't sure if you were tired from the work or still tipsy from the beer. Rodrigo stood in the parking lot and looked into the distance. John had his head on his desk, and you saw his back heaving like a slow piston.

When you got home later, you drank a Coca-Cola and almost choked laughing as you remembered what a panocha smells like.

"¿En qué te ríes?" Mamá asked.

"Oh, it's nothing."

"Pues . . ."

"Hey 'amá?"

"¿Sí?"

"You said my dad fought in the Civil War, no?"

"Muchos salvadoreños sufrieron, mijo, los pobres."

"Did he ever say anything about it?"

"No, nunca. Just that he escaped."

You showered, letting the water, hotter than usual, almost burning, hit you in the face and tickle your eyeballs through closed eyelids. You looked in the mirror and saw it was almost time to shave. You remembered the first time you had to in high school. No one taught you how, so you nicked yourself so many times that the blood fell from your face and into the sink where it mixed with tap water and swirled like a peppermint candy.

As you tried to sleep, you considered jerking off. Meaning you had to: find a comfortable position on your side with the laptop in front of your face; adjust the volume so you could hear anyone walking by; stroke your dick easy so the backboard didn't bump against the wall and Morse code your singleness to your mother who slept in her room down the hall. You finally realized how ridiculous this was.

You laid there and wondered if a family has ever known what they were buying was made by drunks and if Rodrigo had ever killed a man. You then wondered if your father was somewhere similar, teaching a young man everything he knew. You once had a chance to speak to your father after you graduated from high school, but you turned him down out of spite. Colonization, often, is when the worst part of yourself is empowered.

DAY THREE

You arrived at the furniture store and Rodrigo helped a middle-aged Asian man load an entertainment center, one you remembered quite well had been missing several screws, into his car. John stood behind them with a cigarette in his mouth. "I'm tellin' you, you ain't going to find that cheaper anywhere," he said.

And just like any other day in paradise, nothing changed except Rodrigo stopped humming to ask you if you wanted to hang out after work.

"Órale primo," Rodrigo said.

"Where?"

"Una cantina or something."

Any other person and you would've said, "Fuck that." But you had questions for Rodrigo, and the greatest way to make someone talk was over a beer.

"Fasho."

"¿Que?"

"Yes, of course. Sí."

At the end of that day, John's smile was composed of the same vacant lucidity as a crossfaded frat boy as he leaned back in his leather office chair. "Money in the pocket and you know peace, brother," he said through his teeth.

Rodrigo scoffed and called you over. "Motherfucker, me debe pisto."

You saw Rodrigo walk toward your car in those faded jeans, white sneakers, blue polo, and cap.

"Not going home to change?"

"¿Qué?"

"Uh, your clothes," you said as you pinched your moist shirt.

"No, hombre."

You steered clear of Montrose, where you would've been noticed by someone, and coasted near bars you knew you weren't going to like. Rodrigo vetoed two or three.

"Why?"

"They don't let me."

Rodrigo finally decided on that icehouse on Alabama Street, and the two of you sat down and gulped down Coronas as if they were going extinct.

"Imma get a gin and tonic."

"Gin y tonic?"

"Yes, it's a good summer drink."

"SUMMER DRINK," Rodrigo mocked.

Rodrigo noticed you were peeling the labels off the bottles. "¿Tienes novia?" he asked.

"No."

"Pues, vamos a encontrar alguien para ti, eh?"

"Good luck with that. I haven't gotten laid in about a year."

"¿Por qué?"

"I don't know. Ask them. I don't think I'm that bad looking, you know?"

"Claro que no."

"I mean, I'm sorry I don't have the personableness, o cómo se dice, no soy un cachimbón como . . . un tall, skinny gringo asshole."

"Slow down, bicho. Mira, you have to understand que mujeres like control, sí? They like you control them. When una chica say no, quiere decir que no to you, ahorita. Las mujeres like sex también, pero they don't wanna say that. So, you have to be different from los otros perros para que they feel special."

"Well, I guess . . ."

"Tienes que demonstrar que . . . you good at something. Como, como los hombres que bailen bien. The men who dance good get chicas because they think they can fuck good. O, o como when you buy her a drink con expensive tequila, que tienes dinero."

"But I don't."

"You no have to. Just look like it for the night."

"Fuck."

"¿Qué estudias?"

"Trying to become a teacher or whatever."

"Un teacher. Puedes tell them un poema de amor. They like that. It show que you smart and romántico, no?"

You laughed and in your deep tipsiness, agreed. "Holy shit, Rodrigo, that's pretty fucking good."

"Te digo, hombre."

You wondered how much of a coward you seemed to women then, maybe thought how ludicrous you were to ask a woman of anything at a bar. You wanted to stop yourself from diving into a sea of self-loathing, so you changed the subject. You asked, "Where in El Salvador were you born?"

"I was no born in El Salvador."

"But I thought you said—"

"Born in Honduras, pero crecí salvadoreño. Soy salvadoreño."

"Why do you think that?" you asked, to which Rodrigo sipped his cerveza and looked at the label.

"Everything 1 remember is after El Salvador. Vivimos en El Salvador when they take me from mi mamá, they put me in a truck y lloré. When it stop, they put a rifle in mis manos and told me to kill, everyone 1 could. Y yo corrí. 1 run so far, and 1 stopped y cried in a hole in la tierra. 1 kill the first person 1 see."

"Rodrigo, I'm sorry."

"No. No hay de qué. No fue un hombre, it was a boy como yo. 1 shoot him en el estomago, and he died crying por su mamá. 1 watch him die, and 1 do nothing."

You weren't sure what to say. Rodrigo finished his beer and tossed it behind him, and it shattered against some wall. "Que coma mierda todo," he said.

"Rodrigo, just chill. Can you fucking chill right now?"

"No me hables así," Rodrigo said, his voice raised and stern. "¿Por qué hablas como eso? Como un pinche negro."

When you heard that, all the blood rushed to your feet and you had the sudden urge to run away. "What the fuck is wrong with you?" was all you mustered.

"Sabes, my first job in Estados Unidos, 1 peel shrimp por eight hours a day y they hired a pinche negro desgraciado and he sleep all day in the back. Mauricio tell the boss y el negro with three of his friends beat him up after work. No hay justicia, te digo," Rodrigo said. You saw the bartender motion to the bouncer.

"Jesus Christ, Rodrigo. Let's go. You're being ridiculous."

"Vaya pues . . ."

"En serio, let's go," you said, but it was too late. Three men surrounded Rodrigo, and the bartender told you to pay the tab. One of those men placed their hand on Rodrigo's shoulder, and Rodrigo punched him in the neck. The other men wrestled Rodrigo to the ground and kicked him in unison, in rhythm, a violent square dance. Rodrigo didn't scream but accepted the beating in silence before they lifted and threw him into the street. He floated for a second like in a dream. As you paid and apologized, they pushed Rodrigo back as he swung at anything. You walked over to him and tried to calm him, but Rodrigo pushed you away and someone punched him in the nose, and he bled, and you grabbed him and pulled him away. Rodrigo was so heavy. Rodrigo let you lead him to your car, and he slumped into his seat as you looked in all sorts of directions for police and gave Rodrigo a dirty rag for the blood. You started the car and drove. Rodrigo laughed, coughed, and changed the radio to ranchera music.

You asked Rodrigo once if he was okay, and he laughed harder and said, "Que sí que sí que sí que sí que sí," chanting it almost. The ranchera music was loud and obnoxious, and you asked Rodrigo to turn it down. He said, "Que sí que sí que sí que sí," but didn't do anything except lick around his mouth, spread the blood like ketchup around his lips between laughs. "Que sí que sí que sí que sí que sí . . ." Rodrigo pointed in directions, and you drove into them until he laid his palm flat on the dashboard to gather himself and opened the door, walked off into the night, "que sí que sí que sí que sí que sí," stumbled like a wounded lion, "que sí que sí que sí que sí." You let him go because what, in this moment, can be saved? The ranchera that played was about life.

When you got home later, you avoided your mother and went to bed, and it was uncomfortable as if your body was unwelcome to its own rest, so you laid on the floor with the window open so the sounds of the city sang you to sleep with the white noise of ambulance sirens, breaking glass, and a chugging train, "que sí que sí que sí que sí . . ."

DAY FOUR

You arrived at the furniture store with sunglasses and aspirin as your head and body hurt. Rodrigo had already built a pleather recliner. He seemed normal, whistled and worked hard as ever, and even shook your hand when he saw you. Dude even looked younger. *What was he made of?*

"How are you, Rodrigo?"

"Chivo. And you?"

"I'm alright."

"Tú te embolaste, no?" He laughed hard enough for you to be able to see the shiny pink inside his cheeks.

"Oh, yeah. Totally," you answered. You didn't ask what those new words meant to save yourself from an explanation.

You assembled nine chairs that day, and John asked you to translate to this gorgeous Puerto Rican woman. And man was she fucking beautiful, talked with a raspy accent that could lull you into a daze.

"Tell her this table is one hundred pay-sos, no financing," John told you to translate. You told her not to buy it in Spanish, and John nervously scratched his chest.

"¿Todas están malas?" she asked.

"Sí. Todas rotas."

"What? What's she saying?" John interrupted.

"She doesn't want anything," you told him.

"Why not? 100 pay-sos, 100 pay-sos."

"She knows it's $100."

"Then why don't she fuckin' want it?"

"I don't know, man."

"Ask her."

"She doesn't want it," you said. You told the beautiful Puerto Rican woman to just leave, or he was just going to keep shilling terrible tables.

"¿Todas son malas?" she asked.

"Todas."

"100 pay-sos toe-does," John interrupted.

"She knows they're $100." The woman left, and John stomped into his office and slammed the door.

"You talk to her?" Rodrigo asked me.

"Well, yeah. John made me."

"No, hombre. ¿You talk to that princesa puertorriqueña? Dígame que sí. Dios mío, what I do to her." You laughed to get the moment moved along.

Rodrigo turned to you and laughed the loudest you'd ever heard him. It's as if though you two were cool, and nothing had happened. This is when you thought Rodrigo was as unbreakable as he was volatile. How wrong you were.

"You want to drink at mi casa?" Rodrigo asked, motioned a bottle up to his lips with his thumb and pinky stretched out.

You agreed. You had a strange feeling, this feeling of having one more question you felt you weren't going to get another chance to ask.

"Pero, you have to bring something," he added.

"To drink?"

"No, pa' chingar," Rodrigo chuckled. "Que sí, cipote."

You went to the liquor store after work and settled on a small, cheap vodka, but not too cheap, not in a plastic bottle anyways. When you arrived at the address Rodrigo gave you, you got confused, as it was only a storage facility. You drove around until Rodrigo found you.

He lived in a storage unit, and his bed took up most of the space. He seemed to only have two things: next to the bed was a single paint-chipped, black nightstand with a lamp that lit the space like a convenience store at 3 a.m.; in a corner was an altar with an old black and white photo of a woman, surrounded by flowers, coins, candles, and a beaded necklace with an ivory cross. Rodrigo clapped as you presented the vodka.

"¿Hay, vodka?"

"I wasn't sure."

"'Stá bien," he said and took out two mugs from the nightstand.

"I just had a few questions, Rodrigo."

"Cuéntame," he said as we sat on his bed.

"What happened the other night?"

"¿Cómo?"

"You know, Rodrigo. You fucking punched some dude in the neck."

"Ah. Sí," Rodrigo said, knocked back his vodka and served himself some more.

"You could've killed him."

"Pues, if he wanted to fight."

"Doesn't mean you almost kill the motherfucker."

"Violence is violence, Tomás."

"But there's decency and—"

"Palabras, Tomás. Words. No hay dignidad or honor in violence. Lo haces and that's it. You do not fight if you are afraid to die. If you are afraid to die, stay home and die alone."

You felt like you had to dissuade him from this mind-set, that somehow you were going to say something that would show him a light in one rousing speech. That's when you told him everything about your fatherless life, about how he reminded you of a father you were supposed to have. That he could be a better person, above all this. What a dumb moment in your life. Rodrigo didn't seem to notice anyways as he drank the vodka at an alarming rate. You went ahead and asked him that fated question, before he became something else.

"La guerra, Rodrigo. You said you fought in it. ¿Qué paso? How did you come to be here?" You figured his story could reveal something of yours, perhaps.

"Mi papá paid someone to get me. I go home and many people where I live were killed. They kill salvadoreños all the same. Mi papá and mis hermanos survived, and we went to the piles to look for mi mamá. Alli estaba mi mamá, muerta. We took her, but we had no money, so we put her in a blanket and bury her, mi mamá," Rodrigo finished the vodka, and he looked at the ceiling. "I leave after. I don't like it. El Salvador es mi país, but I'm not ready, bicho."

It wasn't the answer you were looking for. Then again, what answer were you looking for, Tomás?

"I'm sorry, Rodrigo," you said, unsure how to undo this moment. "No. No hay de qué. Mi mamá. Ahí estaba. Mi mamá tan bella. Right there Tomás, como una chucha, mi mamá por Dios mi mamá," Rodrigo's words slurred and became muffled as he dropped the bottle of vodka on the concrete floor. The sound of emptiness resonated in your head.

He rested his sunken face into his hands, and he wept. "Mi mamá mi mamá mi mamá tan bella por Dios tan bella puta madre mi mamá mi mamá."

You just sat there. He wept until he turned away and laid down and stopped moving altogether. You said his name a few times before you placed your hand on his back. He twisted his body, lifted his torso, and pushed you off the bed so hard that your chest was still red the next day. You left him to his inconsolable sadness, too afraid to help since you could barely be a man. You had something to say to him that you felt could've fixed everything, you were so sure, but the words eluded you. You didn't have the language.

That night, you showered for an especially long time until your mother shouted, "¡Sácate! You aren't paying a single centavo here!" You wondered how broken a person could be before they were irreparable, and whether or not Rodrigo was simply waiting to die. Is that what a man deserves? What is a man, anyway?

You laid down on the carpet in a blanket and didn't think about anything else as there were no more questions or answers.

DAY FIVE

You arrived at the furniture store, and Rodrigo was nowhere to be found. You stepped into John's office for your paycheck. He handed over $100.

"That's it?"

"What do you mean?"

"You're paying me shit."

"Well, I don't know what to tell you, bud."

"That's horseshit."

"Well, you can do some other stuff for me."

"Like?"

"I got a guy who would like you and your truck to make some deliveries to the ship channel."

"What kind of deliveries?"

"Don't ask."

And that's when you had it. You had to draw a line somewhere in your life. If not then, when? Maybe it didn't mean anything in the grand scheme of things, but maybe you felt like some sort of progress had to be made after what people, like your mom, your dad, Rodrigo, everyone, went through.

"You're an asshole, you know that? A real fucking class act."

"Go back to your broke-ass country then. You can still make some fucking money for however many kids you got if you apologize now."

"Yeah, good luck with this shithole. Go fuck yourself, John."

You walked out and never returned.

At home, your mother, excited, asked how much you made.

"Just one hundred dollars, 'amá."

"¡Ay! Es bullshit!"

"I know, right?"

"Para qué veas cómo nos tratan."

"I was getting tired of that job anyways."

"You will come to work with me, mijo. We will clean houses together, and I will show you how to be a man."

You never went back to the furniture store. If you saw Rodrigo once more, you'd still not know what to say. Is being a man knowing what to say when it needed saying? Who knows? Maybe you needed to leave Rodrigo there, in your past. Or maybe Rodrigo was supposed to come with you, when he was ready? Who knows. You're someone just as stuck in all this.

Tomás, you will never know what to say to Rodrigo, your father, or anyone for that matter. You know that some things in this life just escape words, escape repair, have no meaning beyond being a result of something unchangeable. You're sitting there with information, but what is its purpose?

Tomás, you fool.

THE LAST KNOWN WHEREABOUTS OF RICARDO FALFURRIAS

RICARDO WAKES UP, AND it's the first time he's felt ok about doing it. His throat isn't as dry, and the muscles in his arms and legs don't hurt. He tries to get up from his seat, but he feels it right in his lungs, the need to fill them with the weight of air. It's a feeling he never had when he woke up back home. Here it goes.

The bus driver says they're in Houston, and he's not sure he believes him. He looks outside the big windows of the Greyhound bus, and he sees dirty buildings covered with signs from politicians, tags, piss, and people with no money sleeping in their heavy shadows. *To not have money is one of the worst things in the world,* he thinks. *You won't have food, clean clothes, fun, or people who love you. At least, that's what mi mamá told me before I left. She cried as I walked out the door, her bowled hands collecting tears. I could tell that she knew I'd do it, and that she couldn't stop me. She'd done it herself about my age too, went between whole-ass countries to escape death. I'm sure she'll understand. Go from a shit town to somewhere else and not be a loser? Fasho.*

Even his last conversation in that small town reminds Ricardo why he left that fucking corny-ass place. At the pawn shop across the tracks from where Ricardo lived, the clerk looked at Ricardo's dad's Purple Heart like he had handed in a rock for money.

"Is this real, boy?"

"Yeah, it's real, man."

"I prefer *sir*, son," he said, and Ricardo knew he wasn't playing. "How'd you get this?"

"How you think I got it? My dad got shot for this country. Now you're asking me all these questions."

"Calm down, son. Now, how much you want for it?"

"Well, to me, sir, personally it's worth a million dollars, sir," Ricardo said. *I know how they work, cutting us out for what we're worth. We have to offer ourselves at least double so they can give us just enough. I don't want just enough.*

"Now, son, you know I can't give you that much. I can give you twenty. I got to find a buyer, a place for it in my shop. I have to make money. I'm running a business."

They settled on fifty dollars after Ricardo told the owner his dad died in the Iraq War, having bled to death in the streets of Fallujah. "Al-Qaeda laughed in the bombed-out buildings," Ricardo said. That last part wasn't true, but he didn't care. *He's looking out for himself. He's lying to me, too. Two lies make a nothing, and everyone gets to go on with their lives.*

"I appreciate his service," the owner said as Ricardo walked out. Ricardo laughed.

While everyone else gets off the bus with homes or destinations, Ricardo waits for the bus station to post the schedule for the rest of the week. He bought a ticket to Houston because it was cheap. Now that he's here, he goes up to the ticket lady to buy his next trip to wherever. This one must be extra long because Ricardo wants to get out of Texas, out of the heat, out of here. There's a bus to El Paso, the furthest he can go that isn't north. He doesn't want to go north. He heard there are just more white people who are worse than the ones here because they think they aren't as bad so they feel they don't have to do anything, as long as they ain't as bad as the ones here. That's what Ricardo remembers his dad told him, after boot camp but before he shipped out. *The government didn't tell us exactly how my dad died, something about being classified. My mom cashes in the checks, either way.*

The ticket to El Paso costs $80, the cheapest they'll go if he only does it a day in advance. Ricardo has $93, $50 for his dad's medal and $43 left from all the money he saved up working with his mamá cleaning rich white people's schools. Ricardo reported back to his schoolmates: "Did you know they get to wear whatever they want? No uniforms like the stupid khaki pants and blue collared shirts we wear, like we work here. And like, no police booths." Ricardo asked his English teacher, Mr. Tomás de la Paz, why they do that, "make us dress like chumps, and the police always look at us like we stole something?"

Mr. de la Paz said, "Well Ricardo." He never called him Ricky. "They don't trust you. To dress yourself or care. That, and they want to think they're doing you a favor by making it 'cheaper' on you to wear the same thing over and over again. They don't think you could come to that conclusion yourself. Rather than address the larger systemic issue of poverty, they . . ." Ricardo forgets what he says after that. *Mr. de la Paz is the smartest person I know, but he talks a lot. Maybe he'll get better at it.* Mr. de la Paz always told Ricardo that he believed in him. Ricardo scoffs. *Whatever that means. That I'll change the world. It makes me feel good, but I guess he's just trying to be nice. How can I change the world when I only got thirteen bucks now anyways? Maybe it'll be different elsewhere, where I can wear what I want, and the cops have to go fuck themselves.*

The ticket lady asks how old he is. In his nicest white-person voice, the kind his mom uses when talking to her boss, he says, "I'm eighteen years old, ma'am, visiting home from college." It makes him feel weird when he does that, like the real Ricardo ain't good enough. Sure, he is def not old enough, but Ricardo figures if he's old enough to be made to wear a uniform and talk white, he's old enough to buy a fuckin' bus ticket. She takes his money and hands over a printed ticket that says his bus doesn't leave until tomorrow morning. *What do I do now? I'm broke. I mean, I guess I could go make money. But how do people do that?* Ricardo recalls how his friend, Guillermo, has a dad who works in construction and would ask if he wanted to make some extra money. Ricardo asked his mamá if he could, but she always said, "¿Pa' qué? ¿Pa' qué te trabajan como un burro y te pagan nada? ¿Cómo a mi? No, Ricardo, tienes que estudiar y hacer mejor." *I mean, she's right. But what good is that now? Why would I study at a place that don't trust me anyways? I'd rather get paid. Houston has a lot of construction going on, so they must need people like me, right? Either way, it's just for now and not forever like Guillermo's dad. Like everyone else back in that nowhere.*

It doesn't take long for Ricardo to find a work site. He rides the rail for one stop. He didn't pay and didn't want to push his luck. That, and he feels bad. *But what am I supposed to do? Walk and lose time making money? That's dumb.* The construction site is near a big freeway. The underpass houses poor people sleeping on dirty towels or newspapers next to an apartment complex that looks expensive with shiny Benzes and ridiculously big trucks parked near it. It seems like they're building more expensive places because crews are destroying old homes, their remains lying around. *It's weird. How do you build more places people can't afford when we're dying in the sun? I guess that's how it is sometimes, throw things away to move on.* There are a bunch of brown workers in orange vests lying on the sidewalk. He goes up to them.

"¿Hay trabajo?"

"Claro, joven. Pregúntale al jefe, ese gringo allá."

Ricardo walks over to this white guy with an orange helmet on, studying papers that look like an old scroll.

"Yo, um, got any work?" he asks. The foreman barely looks up at him.

"You eighteen? Es diez and ocho?"

"Uh, yeah. Fasho."

"Well, ahright. You can clear some of the trash and debris and toss it into that trailer with the blue tarp." He made the motions of picking shit up, huffing over to some other spot, and dumping his empty arms free of that imaginary shit, his scroll still under his arm. "Entiendays?"

"Yeah, man. I got it."

"$150 for the day. Cien paysos."

"Yeah, ok."

"Get some gloves and a vest. Any one talk to you other than me, you play stupid, alright? Estupeedough. Got it?"

"Yeah, man. I got it. I got it."

Ricardo gets to it, lugging scraps of walls, roofs, floors, kitchens, bathrooms, living rooms, throwing the bones of homes into a dumpster so they can build over history for different people because the other people aren't allowed to live in these new ones. Ricardo considers how it's kind of scary how long workers get to think about these things as they do them, carrying as much shit in his hands from point A to point B. He feels like that guy Mr. de la Paz taught about. *Systemus or whatever the fuck, the one who rolls that rock up a hill for it to roll back down. Why does he keep doing it? Is it to get paid, like me? I wonder what he gets out of it. I don't know.* The one time Ricardo asked Mr. de la Paz for the answer, he gave his usual bullshit: "It's your interpretation." All Ricardo knows is that no matter how many piles he takes from this hill into the dumpster, it doesn't get any smaller.

Everything hurts. Ricardo can feel it in his arms and legs, between his thighs that are as dry as sandpaper. He tries to drink as much water as his body allows from a grimy-ass orange cooler. Cold water hurts to drink. Slowing down hurts. Carrying less doesn't make it hurt any less. As the hill gets smaller, Ricardo don't feel any better. His head hurts. Breathing hurts. Everything hurts so much that nothing hurts. He knows there's a word for that, but fuck it. *Does something need a word to exist?* It's only when he drinks water that he's reminded of his body. Lifting things and carrying them one place to another is both the easiest and hardest thing to do. *Some people do it forever.*

When it's break time, Ricardo dumps a cup of cooler water over his head and neck. It's 11 a.m. All the Mexicans and Guatemalans and Salvadorans eat separately, sitting alongside a wall away from each other. That weirds him out. *Aren't we the same? How poor we are? How much we don't have? I don't know. I guess not. Do I sit with the Mexicans? The Salvadorans?* Ricardo sits by himself and sips water to distract him from his body's hurt. A man from the Mexican group waves Ricardo over. He wears pants stained with paint like in those paintings Mr. de la Paz showed him once by some crazy white guy.

"¿Tienes comida, joven?"

"No," Ricardo says. He forgot food was a thing. His stomach burns.

The man responds, "Toma." He then hands Ricardo half of his bologna sandwich that sticks to the roof of his mouth with each bite. "Me recuerdas mucho de mi cuando yo fui joven. Trabajando y trabajando."

"Sí," Ricardo says. He didn't catch everything the man said. *He talks too fast.*

"¿Tienes niños?" another man asks Ricardo. He is missing two of his teeth under his bushy, black mustache.

"Sí," he lies.

"Jaja. Yo también. De tu edad. Un hijo." The other man pauses between each couple of words, a life happening again and again in seconds. "Pero ahora? Chiiiiiiin . . . Como seis. Cinco hijas. Un hijo."

"Puta madre, Rolando. ¿Tienes una maldición o qué?"

"¡Chíngate!"

"¿Y tú, joven? ¿Cómo se llama tu hijo?"

"Ricardo," Ricardo says, unable to come up with anything better.

"¿En serio? ¿Como ese cubano mariconcito?" one man asks with a smirk on his face.

"Luuuucy, I'm home!" another man calls out with his head bent back like a howling wolf. They all laugh.

Ricardo doesn't like that he said that. *What did anyone being gay do to him?* Ricardo thinks back when his mamá did this thing where she encouraged Ricardo's liking of girls over boys, this thing where she'd talk about how bad the world is, how some men she knew would beat up other men if there was even a hint of love or sex or intimacy in the way a man interacted with another, that even the idea of one man being affectionate to another caused such an anger to curdle inside of them as to want to hurt another person. Ricardo remembers feeling not being able to ask why. His mamá would just say, "Así es." If he asked again, she'd get mad. Ricardo notices one of the men seeing the look on his face.

"Una broma, joven."

"Sí, solo una broma," another says. Ricardo tries his best to chuckle genuinely.

Then Ricardo says, "Pues, me voy a acostar." He leaves, not even saying thank you or looking at their reactions. He walks to the underpass from earlier and finds a corner to lie down in. His body doesn't hurt as much now that he's mad. He breathes in and looks around. There's another worker laying down in another corner, wearing an orange vest that shimmers with his every move. They meet eyes. They both do the nod, the one Brown people do to each other to make it known that they're there together, not even as friends per se but as a people living this life in the same America. The orange-vested man points in the group's general direction and gives a thumbs down with a scrunched face. Ricardo can feel himself smile. The boss blows a whistle and hollers for everyone to get back to work.

Lifting debris now doesn't hurt so much. Sometimes Ricardo feels the water crawl up his throat, but he keeps it down with deep swallows, each warmer than the last. He can't stop thinking about what they said. *I hate this. I hate how all these buildings are designed and built by people who don't really give a shit about me. School, books, the city, the world. I just want it all torn down and built right, once and for all.* "*Así es*," his mamá would say.

When it's 5 p.m., Ricardo goes up to the white guy to get the money he owes him.

"Hello, sir. I'd like my money," Ricardo says in his white voice.

"What? Oh, yeah. Let me go see what you did."

They walk over to where the mountains of debris were, now just an ocean of concrete with white streaks and peppers of drywall, rusty nails, and paint chips. The white man inspects the space, squatting and eyes bugging out of their sockets.

"Alright, here's the deal. I can pay you the $100 . . ."

Ricardo corrects him, "You said $150 earlier, sir."

"Right, $150." The white man looks annoyed. "I can pay you the $150 now, or I can pay you double tomorrow when you come back and work again."

"Nah, I'm good, sir. I'll take the $150 you owe me now."

The white man takes his helmet off, rubs his bald scalp, then puts it back on. "You sure?"

"Yes, sir."

"Ok, here's the deal," he says with his arms crossed. "Part of why I want you to come back tomorrow is to pick up these nails and stuff. It's dangerous to just have them lying around here. Someone could get hurt. Machine tires get punctured," the white man says, his eyes looking toward the sky.

"You didn't tell me that, sir."

"We said *all* the debris. We can't pay you the full amount if you didn't finish the job."

Ricardo could feel something rising up in him, energy or anger, this feeling to run and run. The white man reaches into his pocket and pulls out a fold of twenties. He shows Ricardo one hundred dollars. His ears burn. His heart beats faster.

"Sir, there's fifty dollars missing," Ricardo says politely.

"Didn't you hear me? I can't pay full for unfinished work." The white man gives Ricardo this look like he's the one making this difficult. "You can take it or leave it, uh-me-go."

Ricardo's shaking. He doesn't remember ever feeling like this. The closest he can think of is when he saw his mamá cry her hardest cry when her purse full of stuff she couldn't get back was stolen: money, papers, precious things from the past. She couldn't even say anything to the police. It's this feeling of not being able to do something while the problem looks you in the face like you're the problem. Ricardo snatches the cash out of his hand. *Así es, así es . . .*

"Calm down. That's honest pay for work."

This is when Ricardo loses it. "Man, fuck that and fuck you. You're full of shit, fuckin asshole."

"Hey! Get the fuck out of here before I call ICE on your illegal ass."

It's here when Ricardo sees this vision play out in his head, where he punches this asshole in the nose and blood seasons the pavement; the sun's light, having traveled millions of miles, dances in its luster. He walks away. The other workers look at Ricardo. *I'll be gone from here soon anyways, go to some place where I don't have to put up with this shit.*

Ricardo walks along the rail because it's his only point of reference in this place, veins of ugly metal. *I'm so tired.* He finds a series of bars and restaurants with white people covered in tattoos and wearing mismatched clothing. There are so many white people inside these bars and restaurants and stores that sell dumb shit. *It's like white people don't do anything here except enjoy shit.* Further down the sidewalk, Ricardo can see Black and Brown people laying down on concrete in mismatched clothing, too. He feels sick. His head hurts as though a bee stings his brain every thirty seconds. He finds an alley that doesn't smell too bad. He lays down somewhere, hidden by a brick wall, using his bag as a pillow, and fades into a haze kind of like sleep.

Ricardo doesn't remember having slept when he's woken up. The person who woke him up is some white dude with a handlebar mustache, slicked-back hair, nice pants, shoes, and shirt, with a huge hole in his ear and tattoos piled up and down his pasty arms. Ricardo sits up and stretches the tiredness out of his joints. *It's strange. I don't remember the last time I had a dream. I lay down and then wake up, like I'm at point A and then point B in the blink of an eye.*

"Damn. What time is it?" Ricardo groans.

"It's 9 p.m., bro."

"Well, shit."

"Listen, pal. We need a bathroom attendant tonight. You in?" he asks.

"How much?"

"Five bucks an hour plus your tips and two domestic drinks. It's a pretty good deal."

He thinks about it. Ricardo remembers his bus leaves around 8 a.m. He has nothing else to do.

"Alright, shit."

"Cool," he says. "And change your clothes. You smell like shit, bro. Follow me."

"Yeah," Ricardo says. *Fuckin' asshole.* He walks behind the white hipster to get to the place he'll be working at. It's nice, the kind of shit you see in white people movies with leather seats like from the '50s and a wall of beer spouts and differently colored bottles of alcohol. The prices are silly, six dollars for a can of piss or nine dollars for bottom-ass liquor with soda. Ricardo questions this paradigm. *Ass-backwards. What can someone escape into with bullshit like that? At least none of this fuckery was in that small town.*

"Over here," the white guy says as he leads Ricardo to the restroom. It's a clean, white bathroom that smells faintly of shit. He thinks of the fanciest word to describe it: *pristine.* So *pristine* that it almost means nothing more than what it is: a place to shit and piss.

"There's your stool and gear. Offer cologne, napkins, mints, whatever. We get busy around 10 p.m. So just hang tight. Got it?"

"Yeah, yeah. Make it nice for white people 'n shit. I got you."

"Uh, yeah. Sure. What do you want to drink?"

"Uh, fuck. A beer, man."

Ricardo roots around in his bag and gets some clean pants and a shirt. He thinks he has a few outfits left before he must clean everything. He changes and looks in the mirror. Ricardo doesn't recognize himself for a second. *Maybe this is a dream, everything so clean and my brain woozy, a blur framing my vision.* But he feels himself breathing. *What if I wake up in my bed? What changes?* He realizes there's music playing real low from outside, white people music. The white guy comes back with the beer.

"Here you go. There's a platter over there to put all the glasses people leave. Bring it to the bar when it's full."

Ricardo sits on the stool, sipping beer and staring at the lights. They're bright enough to be uncomfortable, and they hum without having to stop for breath. He heard that good beer tastes almost like nothing, just enough to remind you it's beer. At least, that's what the older guys said at school. *I guess I get it.* The beer tastes bad. *Crisp, but bad. Maybe because you're just supposed to get drunk off it. Nothing more.* Ricardo does some math. He thinks he's going to be paid for four hours. *So that's like twenty dollars. Plus tips and one more drink. Money is just miles. The more money I have, the further I can get from all this,* Ricardo hopes. He finishes the beer and puts it on the tray, the last gulp bitter enough to scrape his throat on the way down.

They start coming in. They're white and wearing some goofy shit like khaki shorts, a blue button up shirt, and a stupid hat. He can hear them grunt and piss. They finish, zip up, and walk over to vigorously wash their hands. Ricardo goes up to them and offers tissues, mints, cologne, whatever. They take some tissues and try hard to not make eye contact with Ricardo. They drop a dollar and some pennies in the jar. That's pretty much it for a while. Sometimes they want a spritz of cologne or a mint or two, saying thanks. For a while, it's a bunch of white dudes pissing, shitting, doing their best to not know Ricardo exists, and dropping the minimum amount of cash to not feel bad about it. *Fuck you, pay me, I guess.* Ricardo gets a second beer at some point that he chokes down. *The shit that comes out of their mouths is pretty stupid*:

"I know she wants my cock, dude. I know it."

"Is there a cold breeze in here? Must be."

"Shut the fuck up."

"I'm not racist, but they gotta do something about all the homeless people down the street."

"The construction is out of control around here."

"I know! The worst part is all of the workers not knowing English."

"Right? It's not even that hard to know, 'Get the fuck out of the way.'"

Damn. If someone talked this kind of shit in my neighborhood, they'd get knocked the fuck out.

"You remind me of someone I know," one of them says.

Ricardo looks up, and it's some drunk gringo looking at him.

"You want a mint or something?"

"You remind me of someone. Yo, do you know Carl? His name is Carlos, but I called him Carl."

"Uh, yeah," Ricardo lies.

"Oh, shit. I went to college with him! Goddamn! Wait here, man." He comes back with a shot of something and hands it to Ricardo.

"Here you go, man. Cheers!" He clinks the shot glasses and swallows it. Ricardo drinks it, too. It burns. Tears in his eyes. It's like it claws everything on the way down. Ricardo gags. It wants to come back up. Ricardo swallows as hard as he can.

"Haha. Take it easy, man. Fucking Carl." The gringo lumbers back out. *Why do people do certain things?* One time, Mr. de la Paz told the class about how a turtle lays its eggs and then swims back into the ocean, leaving its babies to make their own way. When Guillermo asked why the mother didn't just stay, Mr. de la Paz said it was just what they did, instinct. *Is that what we all have? Instincts? Is that why white people give me free alcohol and take my money? Is that why people like my mom and dad and me just move around?* Ricardo thinks and thinks. He can't stop shivering. He goes out to get a water. *There're so many people, all talking and not caring about people like me.* Ricardo asks the bartender for a water.

"Sure thing. Did you get your second drink?"

"Nah," he lies. *What does it matter?* He gives Ricardo another beer. He looks at some foofy-ass clock on the wall. It's midnight. He goes back to the bathroom.

At this point, there is no such thing as time. Ricardo can't feel anything except the thoughts that flow like honey in his brain. Everything has a blur around it. The lights. The tiles. His hands. The blue of the stalls. All the songs coming from above are chopped and screwed. Like he's in some dream, some dream, some dream. But it's not. Right? Everything wants to come out of him, and it hurts to stand up. Ricardo runs to a toilet and kneels before it, head bowed as though waiting for a bendición. The walls around him spin. Spin. Spin. *Así es. Así es. Así es.* Ricardo remembers this one time when Mr. de la Paz looked him in the eyes and said he could change the world. He seemed like he meant it. *Me?* He throws everything up. His puke hits the toilet bowl with the sound of an applause. *Me? Me?* Ricardo spits out the last bit of acid on his tongue. He gets back to work.

It's all just a bunch of actions for Ricardo after that. Hear piss and shit. Offer things. Be ignored. Coins clink. A door shuts. When the bartender comes in, he takes the cup of tips and spills it all out. He takes some of the cash. *It's something I should probably get used to for now, until I find somewhere that doesn't take a piece of what's mine. That's it.* He gets $42.78. He collects his stuff and leaves before they take anymore.

Ricardo looks at the clock. 2:30 a.m. In his past life, he would've been watching TV or playing some video game. Outside, there are people stumbling into each other, yelling, kissing, staring into the sky. Someone pisses in some corner. Someone else shoves food into their mouth. There's no police. *How weird. This is what it's all for, I guess.* Ricardo doesn't know where to go, but it must be away from here. He walks to the rail and waits. Someone sits nearby, weeping into their hands like his mother did when he left. He wants to be as far as he can. *From all of this. From all of you.*

The rail arrives, the last one. *A robot woman voice tells me I'm not supposed to be drunk. I'm not supposed to be a lot of things.* He sits. There are people throughout the rail car, all looking at something on the floor. Some people are drunk. There are people who just got off work. Ricardo can tell from their clothes and the tiredness under their eyes. He's both. *Everyone is in a trance, far away from here.* He gets off near the bus station and goes inside. He almost expects his mamá to be there, waiting. But she isn't. *Maybe she's forgotten about me already. I don't blame her, I guess. How much did she leave behind to build something better? That's all I'm doing, yeah?*

Ricardo shows his ticket. He buys a sandwich and water for $3.50. They go inside of him. He can feel the chunks of sandwich pile in his belly and dissolve. He sits again. He thinks about how much money he has. About *$150*. Ricardo has a medal or two more from his dad who died in some war. He likes to think this is better than not being anything, if he'd stayed home. *Doesn't matter.* He thinks he sleeps. He's not sure. There's no dream. It's all the same in front of him anyways, hour after hour. There's a sun that rises in the morning. They call to board. He waits in line. No one is really here. Everyone wants to not be here. Ricardo shows his ticket again. He sits in some other seat and waits to leave this place. *There must be something better than all this somewhere, right?*

There's a sky outside the window, and the dirty buildings are still there. Ricardo remembers how everything is built. *Change the world? Ha. Fuck that.* He breathes. The bus pulls from the station. The engine hums as it did the last time, maybe singing something in some language Ricardo can't speak yet. Maybe every engine is telling everyone to keep going farther and farther, away from where you are. Ricardo hears it into yet another dreamless sleep.

THE MANY LIVES AND TIMES OF ARANSA DE LA CRUZ

What we may be witnessing is . . . the end of history as such: that is, the end point of mankind's ideological evolution and the universalization of . . . [a] final form of human government.

—FRANCIS FUKUYAMA, "THE END OF HISTORY?"

ARANSA DE LA CRUZ learned that the worst feeling in the known world was realizing that sometimes, even in your own story, you were not the protagonist. She became aware of this every morning after work when she performed this ritual: put on her faded, nine-year-old shirt from her freshman high school varsity track team and pajama pants; brushed her teeth; looked into the mirror and wondered if the bags under her eyes did not seem too bad; and lay in bed to stare into the vast emptiness of her studio apartment as she struggled to fall asleep, as though she had to relearn how to do it every time.

When someone inevitably asked about the bags under her eyes, she told them the short version of the truth: "I haven't slept well, you know?" What she had not mentioned was that she knew exactly the source of her shitty sleep; her mother, a maid and janitor for the last forty years of her life, was killed when American Airlines Flight 11 crashed into the North Tower of the World Trade Center a year ago. When Aransa's brain finally welcomed rest, she dreamt. And those dreams, which she sometimes remembered like first dates, were never about her. She wrote the ones down that lingered about her consciousness in her journal.

◎

9/11/2002

I wake up standing in a small, white room, and I can't get my eyes to look down. There is a white door. I can only look forward. I walk to the white door, open it to see the side of a staircase and an office space so clean, really clean like my mother would make them. I take a few steps onto a carpet floor, and it warms my feet. I hear a roar or vacuum and struggle hard to look up a staircase, and there's someone sitting, and their head is bobbing like they're weeping. I look to see whose face it is. I want to cry, too. There's the sound of a large monster roaring, and the loudness pools in my ears. The roaring or vacuuming stops suddenly for my mother to yell, "Aransa!" and I wake up.

◎

Aransa's family originally consisted of herself, her younger brother Francisco, and their mother, who all lived in Houston for all their lives until Francisco graduated high school. What with Aransa living on her own and Francisco off at college, Aransa's mother lifted her hands, said "ya!" and moved to New York with her sister to clean office buildings. Her aunt Griselda invited them years ago, but Aransa's mother couldn't accept the offer until she could afford the bus ticket. Aransa asked what difference it made cleaning entire houses in Houston or office buildings in New York. Her mother replied, "Nada." What Aransa's mother had not told her, and wouldn't have even if she wanted to, was that she feared being alone. This was an inherited trait in the family that Aransa hadn't discovered until it was too late: never saying what ought to be said.

By too late, refer to the incident when Aransa put into practice this same flaw when she graduated from high school, started college on a full ride, attended classes full-time for two years, and dropped out to pursue a career in writing. Well, she called it "dropped out," especially to her mother. What actually happened was that she was put on disciplinary probation after getting caught smoking marijuana outside the art school by campus police.

Aransa was suspended for an academic year. Such a deep shame filled her that she made no plans on returning to school. When she worked up the courage and told her mother the truth, Aransa was called a fucking inútil, estupida, and told, "Cállate!" more times than she could count; and as she waved a solid finger in Aransa's face, her mother said that it was a mystery as to how Aransa was born, because "yo no tengo hija." Aransa then learned that to tell the truth forces a person to never feel more alone in their lives. Aransa would not speak to her mother, or anyone else for that matter, for a year. During which time, she tried to read good books but could never concentrate, tried to watch TV shows but could never stand how intentionally ambiguous every ending of each episode turned out, and watched film after film because it was the only way she could process information: 1.5 to 2 hours at a time.

At the end of that year, Aransa had been invited by her mother to come to Francisco's high school graduation ceremony, "pa' que veas." Indeed, Aransa attended and, though she had not intended it, felt even more shame as Francisco swelled with pride while he collected his diploma. After Francisco left for college in Austin, their mother went to New York while Aransa stayed in Houston alone, which goes to show that solitude is a condition that can be inflicted like a slap.

Not too long after, another great shame arrived in a rejection letter from a publisher for her first book of poetry:

Though your method of writing is often quite good, we are looking for someone who can break open the piñata of Hispanic-American ethnic oversimplification.

As soon as she finished reading that letter, Aransa decided that Houston did not let her breathe, was ruining her art, and therefore, killing her soul.

Aransa, too, feared being alone, and her conscious conclusion was to be alone with her mother who once called her, "Aransa mi alabanza." And yes, Aransa was the sort of person to dwell in the past because the present never gave opportunities and the future burned away as soon as it came.

◎

"Hey 'amá, it's me."

"¿Aransa?"

"Si, Mamá."

"Mija."

"Mamá, how are you?"

"Aquí nomas trabajando como siempre."

"Mom, I . . . I want to go to New York."

"¿Por qué? ¿Y tu writing?"

"No sé, Mom. No sé cómo explicarlo. Cómo se dice . . . It's, it's not working out here. I would like to go to New York for just a bit. Para . . . a . . . arreglarme, you know?"

"Aransa."

"Yes, Ma."

"If you come, vas a trabajar," her mother said. Aransa imagined her mother's finger, extended and stiff, poking into the air.

"I understand."

"¿Sí?"

"Yes, Mamá. I will work."

"Ya se acabó tu dream."

"Yes," Aransa said. But like any person who hated defeat like the taste of medicine, Aransa understood that distance from something scraped out the heart for something new; she'd return to Houston someday, but it was not right for her at the time.

So, for nearly two years, Aransa lived with her mother and aunt as they cleaned buildings they would never have an opportunity to make dirty. Aransa decided that when she had had enough, she'd return to Houston and start over.

◎

Aransa forgot what it meant to be alive when she found out her mother died. Because Celia de la Paz was undocumented, Aransa could not prove that her mother's remains were amongst the ashes. And because none of her bosses would affirm or deny that any Celia de la Paz was in their employ, Aransa understood that the only evidence of Celia de la Paz's existence was the emptiness left behind in her soul. So, Aransa learned that even a lifetime of work could mean nothing in an instant, that the story of one's life dissolved in the face of larger, sweeping narratives. The truth, Aransa, is that death has no voice.

Consider the many times when Aransa, a child, would be silenced by her mother against speaking out against the wrongs in the world. Once, a boss underpaid Celia the agreed-upon rate for cleaning their house. "You should say something," Aransa logically posited. "Ay, más problemas," Celia responded. Another time, police came to ask questions regarding the suicide of Aransa's next door neighbor, if they knew anything. They did; the family of Celia, Aransa, and Francisco sat silently in the living room as their neighbor screamed to themselves in the parking lot.

"No, no. I know nothing," Celia said to get the police out of her life.

"Why didn't you say anything about last night?" Aransa asked, Francisco too scared to do it himself, as always.

"¿Y qué? So they can take me? You want to live con un foster family and be separada from your brother?"

"No, mom. Así no trabaja. Hay laws y court y due process y how do you say . . ."

"Pues, cuando tengas el dinero para todo eso, be my guest."

And another time, Aransa asked if she could put her mother's name on car loan applications as a cosigner.

"Que no, hija. I'm sorry pero they gonna look at mis taxes and they gonna find something to kick me out. Ya sabes los gringos."

This was all summed up in one quote Aransa's mother shouted at her once for trying to register her mother to vote for a school project. "¿Por qué siempre quieres involucrarme con el mundo? The world no care about me." It took many years for Aransa to realize that she didn't inherit her mother's fear because she had the privilege of seeing herself with rights.

As it turns out, Aransa's mother was right after all. How can you fight the largest entity in the history of the humankind, especially if it didn't consider you a real person at any point?

Your mother cannot be proved to have existed at the time of the tragedy, the government essentially said on its pristine letterhead. "My mother existed," Aransa said to some faceless government worker on a phone call. "Not according to our records," they said in a calm voice. *She did. She didn't.* Turtles all the way down, as they say. Aransa didn't even have enough money to pay her rent comfortably, fuck a lawyer.

Forever forward, Aransa inherited the burden of her mother's nonexistence when she went to work, returned home, and slept, alive yet not, searching for her relevance in the new epoch.

◎

Aransa did a few things to stop herself from dreaming. She cut back on her sweets and smoking, though she immensely enjoyed the lingering taste of Coca-Cola and cigarettes on her tongue; stopped watching Italian horror films where blood was bright, bright red; she changed the cell phone contact from "Mom" to "New York," in case a call came in. She figured that if such a thing were to happen, she could imagine something like the Empire State Building or a

large slice of pizza on the other side of the line and not her dead
mother yawning from her last sleep.

Aransa loved films. When she finally thought about why, she
figured it was not as a critic but out of love of a primordial solace
she found in even the worst movies. In New York, they were a rare
treat as tickets ran at least the price of three cheap yet filling vodka
tonics she drank alone while her mother slept. Aransa once invited
her mother to a movie as a way of reconciling a fight they'd had the
day before, and Celia responded with a "sácate." Alone, Aransa was
comforted by the ritual of sitting in a tight chair, everything slathered in darkness, and witnessing a story play out before her eyes. It
was a light, the only light, which rested on her clothes and on her
face, projecting characters that lived in a universe somewhat like
hers, where in two hours many lifetimes, crises, hungers, laughter,
sobriety, flaming cars, forbidden kisses, intimate whispers, songs,
bullets, careless tears, soaring mountains, and all their friends came
into being, only to end in blackness with the names responsible for
all of it.

Continuing this tradition in Houston, Aransa went to a shoddy
theater with no real name, just "CINEMA" stamped out in white,
fluorescent letters. Each ticket cost $1.50, and Aransa bought many,
even to knowingly terrible movies, and sat in a torn chair whose
revealed cushion was the color of exposed fat from a deep cut. She'd
wait for another life to flash before her eyes that she would recount
to herself later in bed to keep her mind occupied when trying to
fall asleep.

◎

The New Age
RATED [R]

A man with an empty face sits at a table with a steaming plate of
scrambled eggs in front of him. He walks over to a window to look

at the moon chunks that crashed on Earth months ago. The moon chunks glow like clean skin. He chuckles at the people who fell in love with them and now pray to them for the unborn. The man with the empty face checks on the tomatoes he is growing in the living room.

Cut to: Him shaving. He nicks his chin but is not worried.

Flashback: *A memory of when he nicks his chin shaving the year before. He walks into his job and a co-worker hassles him about how the newer shavers had an update that "didn't do that anymore, you know."* "As much as anything else," the man with the empty face says, "don't do anything anymore, I mean."

The man with the empty face goes outside and passes all the altars of moon chunks. He steps over the meditating acolytes. He does so with a frown. Someone died from praying without eating.

"Celso?" the man with the empty face asks.

Flashback: *They sit in a pre-tomato-infested living room where Celso tells the man with the empty face that his wife is angry that he can't get it up anymore and that his children's eyes hurt because they had to read books to learn. The man with the empty face opens another beer for Celso, and they toast, "A la chingada."*

Another flashback: *Celso invites the man with the empty face to come over and eat flautas that his wife has made. The man with the empty face says no, and Celso promises to save him some.*

The man with the empty face looks at Celso's corpse. Celso is dead and probably so are his wife and his children. His mouth agape and skin as dry as crinkled cardboard, a look of terror in his wide-open eyes as if he had seen every evil in the history of man ever in one glimpse. The man with the empty face moves Celso onto the grass. He retrieves a shovel and drives it into the ground to bury Celso.

The man with the empty face wanders into people's homes. When he loots his adjacent neighbor's house, he sees through the open bathroom door: Phillip's wife sprawled out on the floor, naked. It seems that she had been getting ready for her morning shower long ago, and the see-through curtain with flowery designs covers her. Her breasts and pubic hair are visible, though coated with a veneer of print flowers.

The man with an empty face says nothing and now wears a face with a tone of loneliness we all understand too well. He leaves the house and, in the distance, sees another person looking at him. The man with the lonely face walks toward the other person, and they walk toward him, as though caught in a mirror.

The camera zooms on the man's empty face until a smile erupts.

Fin

◎

Aransa and Francisco rarely, if ever, talked in their entire lives. After their mother's death, Aransa de la Cruz and Francisco de la Paz (Aransa took her father's last name, Francisco their mother's) only talked once about the whole thing. Aransa processed the awkwardness the best way she could, in a poem.

THE DAY AFTER MOTHER DIED

My brother and I discussed if we
cared to know each other anymore.
"No sé," he said. "Me neither," I said.

We stared in each other's eyes. I
had to forget he saw me get popped
in the mouth for letting a boy run

his hands up my leg. Mamá was outside
pulling the head off a chicken so well
that I wondered how we went hungry.

She used those hands to put the fear
of Hell in me. We left without a word.
There is a building made of mossed-

over bricks with hundreds of people
living in rooms with TVs tuned
to different channels. Once in a while,

one of those people might knock on
another's door and look into the peephole
until it darkened, knowing someone

was staring back, not knowing yet whether
they were going to be welcomed in.

Aransa wrote it on her shift at her new job at Hobby Airport. She applied and received the position while in New York and didn't tell her mom until days before she left. Aransa could never remember the title of the position, but it required her to walk down the aisles of a parking garage and check the license plates into a system for expired parking passes.

Her shift was from 10:00 p.m. to 6:00 a.m., and her feet swelled with blood on the first night. Cleaning office buildings at least allowed her to sit once in a while. Luckily, she had gotten used to creeping fatigue and usually finished a level in half the time it took when she first started. In those first three months, rather than finish early and be assigned another level, Aransa took to writing poems and notes on her clipboard while riding the inter-terminal tram that hummed as it glided on its rails. It was best at 4 a.m. when seldom was anyone there. "Silence is an emotion. / A rail erases a secret / written in lamp oil / along its tracks . . ." she wrote. However, her sleeplessness was difficult to adjust to on account of the parking garage's gray walls that indicated neither night nor day. But such loneliness also welcomed the imagination as Aransa often felt the presence of an aura pressing against her brain like a damp cloth. In the corner of her eye appeared a fuzzy ball, a wavy line, a garbled cloud, a rustling dot, and, if she thought too much, the potential of rape, a stabbing, a goopy presence seeping out of a Toyota Tercel's muffler that could grab her leg and devour her body to liquefy her internal organs all increased. The fear tired her beyond belief.

But of course, after her mother's death, such an imagination ended as soldiers roamed the airport halls. Her peaceful rides on the tram were ruined by men in green camouflage and tactical vests who sat in gray and blue seats while M16s rested in their hands. Her walks in the garage were no longer ones of heavy solitude as the huffing of dogs and the garbled language of radio static were heard in the distance. For Aransa, it was the sort of loneliness that only felt more apparent than ever as the soldiers' routine treated her existence as an accessory, akin to a stereotypical character who helps a white protagonist in the films Aransa tried her best to avoid. The heroes never looked like her. They never shared the same defeats as her, their victories unfamiliar and strange to Aransa. Often, the films made it seem that it was Aransa's duty to accept and love their flaws as sexists or racists; if she didn't excuse that, then she couldn't watch any fucking movie. When a movie finished, she felt some sort of emptiness at knowing she hadn't found herself by the end while everyone else moved on satisfied. The soldiers acted as they wished around Aransa, but she had to conduct herself accordingly under their presence. It was something she felt foolish to think about, but death creates a vacuum that swallows every other feeling with an efficiency that makes one wonder how narrow existence can become.

That morning, Aransa felt the wet pages of her life dissolve between her fingers. She slept.

◎

9/20/2002

I wake up in a really stiff chair on an airplane mid-flight, and to the left of me sits a woman nursing a baby. I look down to see I have a suit on. Black, real nice, shiny almost. I hanker for a vodka tonic and call the attendant over. She is pretty and has a mole on her cheek that disrupts the clear sky's light on her face, and boy is she pretty. I wait for my vodka tonic, and I can already taste the bitterness. My mouth waters, and I shiver in anticipation. I remember it is my favorite drink in real life, too. I see people I recognize, but I don't say anything to them, as I think we all know we are here, and the thoughts they are thinking are that we shouldn't care to do anything about not knowing each other. The pretty, so pretty, stewardess comes back with her face and then the plane shakes real hard. I look outside the window and below is a glassy city that the blinding sun makes nearly invisible, surrounded by the sea. The plane doesn't stop shaking, and it goes into a slow nosedive. I can't breathe. I look around and everyone's mouth is wide open and only the sound of wind comes out. Then I hear a hollow thud. Next thing I know, the cabin is flooded, and I rise above the water. My head hits the ceiling. I breath in as much as I can until the water fills to the top. I wake up as the water reaches my mouth, wondering if there is a give and take with how disappointed we can be with how we die.

◎

So yes, in the present, a little over a year after her mother's death, Aransa wanders the streets of East Houston and becomes dizzy from looking down a street that seemingly never ends. This time, Aransa forgot her cash to pay for a movie ticket, and they don't accept cards. She goes to a nearby coffeehouse to pass the time. She looks around for a seat and notices a woman lift two fingers and flick them at Aransa. Aransa tries not to notice, but the woman points at her directly and nods. Aransa scrunches the muscles in her face and starts to walk away. The woman calls out, "Hey, you!

Black hair, some sort of Latina or whatever. Girl. Hey, you!" Aransa turns to her, wondering if she has met her but forgotten; she has forgotten many people.

"Hey. Like, hey. Yes, you. Lips right off a Disney princess. Hey." Aransa starts licking her lips and wonders if the woman didn't say her name out of not knowing or as an inside joke they share.

"I didn't mean it like that. Hey. I mean, you have a nice butt like you walk a lot. Just come here." Aransa laughs, then walks over to the woman.

"My hair's not black, it's actually a really dark brown," Aransa says.

"Fair enough," the woman responds. Aransa thinks she doesn't seem too much older than her, perhaps by three or four years. *Maybe she is a college friend*, Aransa wonders. The woman is wearing a black, half-zipped hoodie with a white T-shirt underneath and jeans frayed a bit at the hem. Aransa posits that she is of Asian descent. Aransa thinks she can tell the difference between a Salvadoran ("bien gachos," her mother would say) and an Argentinian ("always con su nariz por arriba"). She couldn't distinguish which Asian ethnicity, though, thinking back to when her family lived alongside an Asian community in a poor apartment complex in Kemah. The woman is pretty like the stewardess in that dream.

"I'm sorry, but do I know you?" Aransa asks.

"Oh, no. I just wanted you to sit with me," the woman says.

"But I don't know . . ." Aransa angled her head to the right.

"We can fix that. Just sit."

Aransa looks around, then sits.

"Cool. What's your name?"

"Aransa."

"Nice."

"And yours?"

"Robin. But call me Bobbi. With an *i*."

"Why didn't you just introduce yourself like a normal person?"

Bobbi scrunches her eyebrows at Aransa, mouth slightly open. "Hey, just chill."

"I'm sorry. Bobbi, what kind of Asian are you? I can tell you're Asian. Like, I just don't know what kind."

"What kind of Asian? Are you serious? I mean, I am. But don't start out with that shit."

"You pointed out I was Latina, so I thought—"

"Yeah, I was just trying to get your attention. But how do you know I'm not Latina?"

"Damn. You got me." Aransa then feels ashamed for asking the question and thinking like this, compartmentalizing others to have some foolish notion of awareness.

"I'm not though, to be clear."

"Bien cute," Aransa says to end this line of conversation.

A waitress comes by and places Aransa's latté on the table in front of her.

"Thank you," Aransa whispers.

"You like coffee?" Bobbi asks. Unprepared for the question, Aransa puts both hands on the cup and looks into the foam.

"I . . . I guess. It's fine. I mean . . ."

"Well, Aransa, I sell cosmetics."

"Oh. I don't want any," Aransa says, defeated. She starts to push herself away from the table.

"I'm just saying. Trying to start a conversation here. Stay. Please." Aransa pulls her seat back to the table and places each hand on each cheek.

"Oh. Door to door?" Aransa asks.

"Yeah. It fucking sucks. You really have to bullshit people and play on their insecurities. So it's always just a bunch of older women who want to be younger, and I gotta tell them the stuff I sell will do that, and they buy it like it's some secret."

"So that's how you knew about my lips."

"Ha. Yeah. You lick them a lot," Bobbi points out. Aransa covers her mouth with her right hand. "I always feel like shit afterwards because I lie to these women and they think I'm saving them."

"That sounds like a lot. I'm sorry," Aransa says.

"You say that a lot. You say something enough times, and it loses its meaning."

Aransa almost says that she is sorry.

"Bobbi, why did you call me over?"

Bobbi licks the inside of her cheeks.

"I thought it'd be cathartic."

"How?"

"This one time in South Korea, I went inside a restaurant, and this dude called me over like I did with you. I thought he was just gonna flirt. He paid for my meal and everything. But instead of like a date or something, he talked the whole time about how he fell in love with someone in Thailand and how he tried to bring him back to the States but couldn't afford to. He was sweaty and shaking, but he seemed relieved. Cathartic, you know?"

Bobbi sits there and looks at Aransa, unshaken.

"Are you trying to tell me you fell in love with me and want to sweep me away?"

"Oh, nah," Bobbi laughs, and Aransa has to cover her mouth again to keep the coffee from dribbling out of her lips. "But seriously, no. It just seems like you have emotional baggage or some shit. You can just talk to someone, you know. Like right now."

"Even if that were the case, you'd be crazy to think I'd tell you."

"Maybe," Bobbi says. The waitress returns and places a large mug of beer with a tint of red in it in front of Bobbi.

"What the hell is that?"

"It's a michelada. I thought you were Mexican or some shit."

"Well, yeah, but I didn't see that on the menu."

"I know the people here, so they made it for me. I met them . . ."

"Bobbi, I have to go to work. Will you be here tomorrow?"

"Yes."

During her shift that night, Aransa notices that the soldiers have finally left the airport, abruptly and without notice. Aransa goes about her shift slower than usual that night. At one point, she hears a muffled cough in the distance. On the fifth cough, she sees a dark figure peer over cars, and a sigh slips out of her throat. Aransa does her best not to fall asleep later, for fear of a nightmare, but fails.

◎

10/5/2002

I'm a woman who resembles my mother staring into a mirror, feeling fresh wrinkles on my neck. I look into my dark brown hair for gray strings, and there they are, like faraway rivers. The mirror is in a clean bathroom, and my hands are rubbery, with thick veins and nails opaque with zinc deficiency. The bags under my eyes are concave enough to collect tears, nearly purple against the backdrop of a yellowing face. My skin is nearly dry and looks like it would only take a tug to peel the epidermis off the bumpy, corn-colored fat underneath. With a single, shaky finger, I pull my mouth apart. A tooth falls out, clanging into the sink. The rest of my teeth begin to drop out of their sockets. I make a nest with my hands to catch them, pale blood leaking through my fingers. My pupils brighten and start to disappear, the mirror in front of me blinding. I wake up and the wall near my bed is so white that I have to reach out and touch it to see if I'm really awake.

◎

Aransa receives a call from "New York":
   "Hello, Mamá?"
   "Yes? Ara?"
   "Hey 'amá."
   "Mija. Dígame. ¿Cómo estás?"
   "I don't know, Mamá."
   "Dígame."
   "I've been having, cómo se dice, nightmares, you know, dreams malos."

"Pesadillas, mija. Te dije. Estop eating sugar. I don't know por qué I have to keep diciéndote."

"No, mom. It's not that."

"Sí, I know. Ay, Ara I keep diciéndote."

"They're just a lot of weird pesadillas, 'amá. No es azúcar, mom."

"Did they have agua in the dreams?"

"Yes."

"Eso significa que algo malo will happen, mija."

"Another one had me wake up a bunch of times in an office building, and I thought I heard you call out to me."

"Pero mija, agua is very bad."

"That was just one, though."

"No importa."

"In that one, I get out of the water a little. I think I still die, though."

"Ah! You get out."

"Yeah, just my nose though."

"Pero despiertas breathing . . ."

"Sí."

"Estarás bien."

"That's good to hear."

"Sólo que you no dream about teeth falling out."

"Oh."

"But you wake up in the other breathing? ¿En agua pero respirando?"

"Yes."

"Good. Ojalá que estes bien."

"I love you, Mamá."

"Sí."

Aransa can't fall back asleep, so she goes to see a matinee.

◎

The Date
RATED [PG-13]

A man and a woman are in the back seat of a taxi. There is no talking. Her head is in his lap, and the man brushes her hair out of her ear with his fingers. The man rests his head against the window as the neon signs of a living city flicker on his five o'clock shadow. The white noise consists of engines, ambulance sirens, tires going over cracked asphalt and speed bumps, lulling the couple into a shared daze. Dew fogs the taxi windows. The man looks down at the woman and finds her staring back at him with love. They sigh in unison as the taxi crosses a bridge. He dips down and playfully bites her nose. The car careens off the bridge and lunges into the ocean. The man manages to escape the taxi, completely submerged in the womb of the sea.

He thinks back on his life.

Cut to: A boy lying in a field as day turns to night, a farmhouse out in the distance.

Cut to: A funeral where there is a large photo of a man and a woman on their wedding day. A teenage boy stands idly by as people console him.

Cut to: A young man in college graduation regalia driving home alone.

Cut to: A man in business casual clothing sitting at a desk looking outside a nearby window, visibly content.

Cut to: A man in casual clothes kissing a woman in a dark bar, the music deafening.

Cut to: A man swimming upward in the backdrop of a midnight blue sea.

He desperately flails upward. The man only sees whiteness until oblong apparitions of the distant figures that must have inhabited the Earth long before humanity soar years above him. He stops swimming, starts floating, the ocean suspending him as though weightless. He wakes up. It was a dream. He is sitting in that taxi with his love still in his lap.

Fin

◎

Before her shift that evening, Aransa goes to that coffee shop to talk to Bobbi.

"Bobbi. Do you still talk to your mother?"

"Yeah."

"How is she?"

"She's good. Won't stop yelling at me. I don't think she has stopped since I was a kid, though. She also hasn't stopped watching the news. Nothing but tributes or remembrances."

"I mean, it wasn't that long ago."

"Yeah, but I don't want see that again. You watch one tragedy, and you've seen every single one at the same time."

"Yeah, but each one is tragic in their own way."

"I guess. My father died in the Persian Gulf War. We were told he died in a missile attack and, you know, you think how he must've both seen it coming and not. And for like that split second, he's every person that was ever huddled and waiting for death to come or not. I mean, death is always a possibility, but they know death is especially likely, and so all they can do is hold their breath and wait."

"I don't think I'd be scared to die if I knew it was coming."

"What do you mean?"

"I think death is just an extension of being alone. I'm used to being alone, and I can take being alone forever if I have to."

"Wait, I've never asked. What do you do?"

"I work at the airport."

"Doing?"

"It's really dumb. I'd rather not say."

"If you clean toilets, that's cool. I can respect that."

"No, sort of a parking attendant. I check license plates to see if they're registered."

"You give tickets?"

"Yes."

"You asshole. How long?"

"It's been about a year maybe."

"Ah. Before that?"

"I lived in New York."

"Go on . . ."

"Let's just say I used to write. When that didn't work out, I moved to New York. Then, life didn't work out in New York. So, now I'm here."

"Moved twice, huh? And you said you write, like, books?"

"Poems, to be exact."

"Cool. Why?"

"I don't know. I guess I've always been a writer. I think a lot."

"We all do."

"No, I mean I think A LOT. To the point that if I stay in my head too long, I go crazy. In fact, if I don't write, I get this cabin fever feeling. I *have* to write is how I'd put it."

"I wish I could do that."

"Do what?"

"Stay in my head. I don't do it at all."

"It's not too hard," Aransa says. Bobbi doesn't respond this time, so they sit in silence for a moment.

"Aransa, I think I'm going to Mexico," Bobbi finally says.

"Why Mexico?"

"It seems like a nice place. I don't want to stay here. Things'll only get worse."

"I see what you mean. Is that it?"

"Well, I talked to my mom, and she started crying all of a sudden um telling me that uh um she doesn't know what I'm doing with my fucking life and uh she's scared that I'm going to wander for the rest of my life and that I won't ever understand peace. She started hiccupping from crying so much and that she doesn't want to die knowing I'll be alone and without having known peace um she said I should stop wandering around because I've actually moved nine times within the last year. She's right, I mean I don't think I know what I'm doing with my life, so I think I'm just um going to Mexico to think about it for a while. Maybe kiss a woman right on the lips, walk in cities of . . . of heat and stone uh climb a mountain or two and I'll maybe meet someone and tell them um I love you so much my legs melt, and I'll want to cry."

Bobbi and Aransa sit in silence for another few minutes, sipping at their drinks. Aransa speaks first.

"Bobbi, you think parents have kids knowing that they aren't perfect themselves? Like, would they have had us if they knew?"

"Shit, I mean, we're here, aren't we? What does it matter?"

Aransa returns to the coffee shop the next day, and the day after, and the day after, not knowing yet that Bobbi will never return.

◎

Another call from "New York":

"Aransa!"

"Yes, Mamá."

"I have something to tell you."

"I'm listening, Mom."

"You are going to be alone for a long time, mija."

"Why?"

"I can't tell you. Pero, you have to know that you will always be loved more than you will be alone."

"Mamá, why are you telling me this?"

"Because it is the only thing you will get free en esta vida, Aransa mi alabanza."

"New York" hung up, but Aransa kept the empty phone to her ear.

◎

On her shift, Aransa wonders if some of the owners of the cars have died since she started working there.

On her drive home after her shift, Aransa sees the highway lanes as film reels.

On her drive home after her shift, Aransa writes a poem in her head:

She threw away her favorite fruits,
squeezing them first, hard enough
to make them bleed.

She stopped answering the phone
and slept like a heap of garbage
waiting to be retrieved.

When I asked, "what's wrong?"
she said, "everything," then
that if she could, she'd

gather every child in the world
separated from their mother
and hold them close,

run her fingers through their hair,
dress them with plenty of buttons
to look them in the face

and smile while fastening them snugly,
glistening spit sticking to their lips
and their head nodding up and down.

Later, I found her lying on her side. When
I called her Mom, she didn't turn. When
I shook her, she did not stir. There's
a rotting stench of sweetness.

Something has to give, someone has to say something, Aransa thinks.

◎

The day before she left for Houston, Aransa de la Cruz opened the door to her aunt's apartment in Brooklyn with groceries after her high school cleaning assignment and called out for anyone home.

"She asleep," Aransa's aunt Griselda said. She sat at the kitchen table reading magazines.

"No she isn't, tía," Aransa responded and walked past her.

The bedroom door was clean and white with a gold-colored doorknob. Aransa clutched the groceries closer to her body. She breathed deeply before entering. Celia de la Paz lay on the floor next to a bed on her side facing a white wall. The curtains were drawn.

"Mamá," Aransa whispered. No response. "Mom, please."

"¿Qué, mija?" Celia groaned, as though uttering took great energy from her body.

"Tía tells me you aren't eating," Aransa said. Celia did not respond. "Why aren't you eating?"

"Hm?" Celia heaved. Aransa made sure the brown bag of groceries crackled in her hands.

"I went to la bodega and got you your favorites, 'amá. Mangos, papayas, some piña." Celia still did not respond. "Mom."

"No seas cruel, mija. Rub my feets. It hurts."

"You know, I think Tía Griselda would be ok with you on the bed for now," Aransa said as she kneeled at her mother's feet.

"Sí."

"Don't you want to move up to the bed?"

"Porfa, mija," Celia pitifully moaned with her eyes closed. Aransa mushed her fingers into Celia's feet.

"Mom, you can't go on like this."

"¿Cómo que no? Not much else en esta vida."

"Oh, Mom, you big dummy. That's not true."

"Ah. Ay mija, what can I do?"

"At this rate, all you can do is die."

"¿Y qué? I think about dying a lot. Y when you think about death as much as yo, it starts to mean nothing."

Aransa didn't look at Celia's face and instead focused on kneading the sole, moving up the arch, and squeezing the ball of the foot and in between the digits. Celia said nothing but breathed through her small nostrils. A grand blanket covered her body from ankle to throat. Aransa stopped to rub her own nose with her wrist.

"Porfa, mija. No seas cruel. Don't estop."

"Mom, what are we doing?"

"Hm?"

"What are we doing here?"

"I've died a million times in my head. I do not worry about such babosadas."

"What about me? Francisco? Are we babosadas?"

"What about los dos? The dead have no childrens."

Aransa de la Cruz would not eat for two days after that and waited fruitlessly for an explanation. In her non-hunger, Aransa went back to Houston. She finally understood that sometimes, people must leave to do what's best for themselves. Even if it hurts.

◎

In the Night
RATED [R]

Xitlali is a spiritual medium who responds to a house call, believing this to be another typical case of the supernatural. Xitlali arrives and Doña Valdez waits out in the cold night. Xitlali enters their apartment and turns on the light. The apartment is small and as she inspects it, she sees that all the pictures are warped and worn and that all the crosses on the walls hang loose, ready to fall.

Toward the back of the apartment, there is a single door that is white and seems to be breathing. The wood strains and relaxes on its squeaky hinges. She taps on it. The frame around the door creaks as though responding to being felt; it seems to have a layer of skin. Xitlali picks at the door until the white scrapes off, and a red tendon glows with blood underneath. Blood trickles to the floor, then flows to the other side of the door. She swings it open, and there is only a brick wall. She sprinkles water from a small jar in her pocket that makes the brick ripple.

When Xitlali closes the door, a fat fly works itself out of the hole she made and takes off into the air. It is loud and frantic, hitting the door violently until it falls to the ground where it struggles. Xitlali steps on it. She lifts her foot, and the fly still thrashes so she steps on it again and again, using more force on each stomp. The final time, she grunts with all her strength, and the fly is flat and moist. Looking closer, she sees a squishy worm rise from the black corpse and wriggle out to escape. Xitlali captures it in a box for further purification.

As she steps outside, she asks Doña Valdez to hold her hands to pray.

Fin

◎

On this latest drive home in the dark morning after her shift, Aransa witnesses the car in front of her get swiped from the left by a large, black truck that sends it swerving about all four lanes of I-45 and into the concrete lining of the freeway. The black truck speeds off into the twilight as if it never happened. Aransa pulls over and calls 911. She runs over to the demolished car and looks to see if the driver is okay. She is not. Her arms and head rest on the deflated airbag. When Aransa calls out to her, the woman in the demolished car turns to look into Aransa's eyes. She has a thin, red line dividing her face into two halves, and she cries and her mouth vibrates, bubbles of blood forming and popping. A clicking sound resonates in her throat. Aransa backs away and peeks over the freeway railing downward and becomes dizzy, realizes that even if she wants to, she can't save the woman in the car or anyone for that matter, doomed to forever be the secondary character in her story if she continues to not want to dream or dwell in the hueco that is her mother's death and remember that protagonists must have a purpose beyond simply existing. She tells the police all of this. It felt right to say something, instead of leaving when she could have. *The first spoken word will inevitably lead to other words, right?* Aransa reasons.

After the police finish questioning her, Aransa drives home to sleep, but not before writing the ending to a poem:

a language only few spoke
who, in their desperation,

looked into sky, to ground,
to someone who might coo

hello.

Aransa wakes up as the sun sets and knows that nothing is too late. Aransa deletes her mother's number from her phone, knowing there will never be an explanation—that is the nature of death—and plans to call Francisco to discuss how she doesn't know what she's doing and how he must not know either because healing is a process and that family curses are an accepted truth until accepted no more. What matters is that something is said.

The phone call will start with, "Hello," and end with, "I love you, too."

Then, years later, Aransa will have one more dream. Until then, she takes the first steps to set her life back on track, back to talking to people and participating in the world, writing poems like she used to. The dream will be:

I look up, and we're in a line with our hands tied behind our backs. There are men shouting orders, and it feels like we've been walking for a long time. Our clothes are dirty and torn, hanging off of our bodies like tissue. There are trees all around and the heat swells our pores. We sweat like ham out of the oven. We walk into what seems to be camp and the children are separated from the adults. I look up, and the sky is smothered in smoke that converges into an eye.

THE FATES OF MAXIMILIANO MONDRAGÓN AND YZOBEAU PONCE INTERSECT IN ACAPULCO

YZOBEAU PONCE INHERITED THE Lunar. The mole emerged in between her eyes like an island of ash in an ocean of sand the morning after her sixteenth birthday. When she glanced into a silver puddle of rain on her way to school, the first vision the Lunar bestowed was a first-person perspective of someone watching their hands slowly dissolve speck by speck and float up into a red sky. It wasn't until after her tenth vision came somewhat true a few years later that she realized the Lunar was actually showing bits of reality, though she wasn't aware of which reality exactly. The vision was of her and her father jumping into a rose-white truck to escape her town after government soldiers began firing into crowds of people; however, in the reality she experienced, she ended up jumping into the bed of a green truck alone. As far as she understood, there's only two realities: things either came true or didn't.

Life passed, and Yzobeau made it as far as Acapulco, Mexico, where she learned to use the Lunar to get everything she needed from strangers: food, shelter, a TV, alcohol, drugs, etc. What she didn't realize is that those same people, though distracted by the visions, still remembered it was her who put them under a spell. Her tactic of entrancing chumps with her Lunar and taking their belongings caught up to her when she did it to the wrong person. Gabriel Aceves, a member of a burgeoning cartel, saw himself in a suit being inaugurated as a politician. He interpreted this as destiny. She swore to herself to make sure that that reality didn't come to pass. Until then, Yzobeau showed her third eye to Aceves's high-profile clients for a high price. This all led to the death of U.S. Rep. Santiago de Luz.

Thus, Maximiliano Mondragón, a journalist, is offered the Acapulco assignment because there isn't much else to do with his fucking life.

"The hell is the Acapulco assignment?" Max asks.

"Former Rep. Santiago de Luz found murdered in a fancy hotel called the Agua Clara, room 501, in Acapulco, Mexico, while on vacation."

"Why do we care?"

"He repped District 143 here in Houston, the ship channel. Could be a link to rising drug-related crimes here. Could be a big story. You want it or not?"

It takes Max a single second to think about everything in his life up to that point before giving an emphatic yes, not considering that the possibility of meeting his death is high, not asking why he was chosen specifically since Max only has an elementary grasp of ess-pan-ol. The truth is that no one else is foolish enough to take the assignment. But what informs Max's decision the most is the fact that his girlfriend of six years, Magda, told him that she did not love him anymore.

Just two weeks ago, she sat him down in a coffee shop in Montrose, told him, stood up and walked away while Max was mesmerized by the sway of her glorious hips once again. *That's what you'll miss until it hurts. You fucked it up somehow you idiot.* Dramatic? Absolutely. But Magda was wired to do shit like that, and Max loved her for it, especially when she covered her face when bright blood bubbled from a wound in a horror film, or when she played Pink Floyd on the record player during sex.

"I don't think *Dark Side of the Moon* was meant to be a soundtrack for fucking, Magda."

"Don't call it that," Magda whispered as she welcomed him into her embrace.

She wouldn't whisper anything to him anymore.

"Yes, yeah, I'll do it, definitely," Max says.

◎

Max arrives at the Hotel Agua Clara in a Volkswagen Beetle taxi, white body with blue fenders, whose driver blasts Guns N' Roses; his name is Emilio, and Max asks him if he knows anything regarding the murder of Rep. de Luz, flashing a two-hundred-peso bill, knowing it speaks volumes more than his shoddy Spanish. Emilio continues to look forward with his hands gripping the steering wheel.

"No, no tank you."

"No tay goosta deenayro?"

"No me gusta problemas," Emilio says into a chuckle.

"Fair enough."

Emilio drops Max off at a hotel that stacks alongside a stony mountain not yet devoured by the sea it neighbors. It is an old-style Mexican building with pseudo adobe walls, brown tile, Virgen statues the size of children blessing every doorway, and the vast Pacific Ocean humming in the background. Of course, the most beautiful and endearing aspect of the hotel is its connection to La Quebrada, a gulch where clavadistas climb the 115-foot cliff to jump off the top and dive into the crashing water below. Max walks over to the clerk, a man in a black and white uniform.

"A room please."

"How many?"

"I'm alone," Max says, the words tasting terrible coming out.

"It's 815 pesos a night, sir."

"How's it so cheap?"

"Not too many people come around anymore, sir."

It's true. Max looks around and sees the rustic halls of the hotel empty and large because no bodies are filling them.

"Why is that?" Max asks, knowing damn well why.

"Well sir, the economy isn't doing too great."

"Right."

"Newspapers are free of charge to guests. Perhaps you'll get to know more from there."

Max looks at the clerk's name tag.

"Look Raúl, I'm going to be honest with you. My name's Sam Gutierrez," Max says, slipping a five-hundred-peso bill over the counter and into Raúl's personal space. "I'm just here to have a good time, if you know what I mean. I'd appreciate if you'd let me know if any police come by."

"I don't think that will be an issue."

"Then just let me know if anything strange walks in. Here's my personal number."

Max enters his room and sits on the bed. He places his palms over his face and breathes deeply, exhaling more air than inhaled. The clink of glasses echoes outside his window. Max lies down on the stiff hotel bed and tries to get his shit together, running achy fingers through his thick yet short hair, eyelids flickering. Every time Max gets his brain to focus on something, he only thinks of Magda and how she lives her life without him. A peephole in his mind's eye creates a single light surrounded by blackness; he sees her laughing and sleeping alone or with someone else, not having to think these thoughts.

Max opens his eyes and sits up. He's been in Acapulco only four hours now. In fact, nothing feels different than any other city until he pulls the starchy motel drapes apart and a heavy night air blankets him. He loves the wrought iron, glassless windows here; they save him time since he opens his window at night to replace

Magda's sleep breathing with the moans of passing cars and the far-off ranting of the sleepless. Now, it is simply the ocean shivering at the moon's touch. The only direction he has is the story about former Rep. Santiago de Luz's death most likely at the hands of a cartel enforcer, possibly related to the rising drug violence in his home district, 143, the very one de Luz represented, and the story is due in forty-eight hours.

◎

Before he can be debilitated by the weight of his solitude, Max makes his way to room 501. He feels a grip on his heart as soon as he arrives at the 5th floor; the cleaning woman is making her way down the hall. Max approaches her.

"Ma'am, I'm sorry but I left something in this room over here, and I need you to let me in."

"I do not let anybody in, señor."

"No, no, no. You don't understand, my boss is right up in my ass about this, and I really need to get what I left. I can either start making some calls, or you can let me in, help me out, take these two hundred pesos, buy yourself something nice, and we can get on with our lives. ¿Comprende?"

The cleaning woman, visibly annoyed, takes the money and lets Max in.

"Pero rápido, sangrón," she mutters.

The room is clean and appears as though nothing ever happened in it. Max searches under the bed, in the closet, drawers. Nothing. Someone cleaned up real nice in the short time since Rep. de Luz's body was lying there not forty-eight hours ago. Max scans in between the bed and nightstand and finds that a small area of the carpet is darker than in the rest of the room. It is not that the stain is completely gone but that the bed is strategically placed to make sure it is not as visible. After moving the mattress frame, Max sees the shadow of a great continent of blood that must have been where

Rep. de Luz's body leaked all its fluids. Max notices that the stain stops just before where the carpet meets the wall. He lifts the tuck and finds a gold ring. The cleaning woman knocks on the door, and Max shoves the ring into his pocket to ponder about it later.

"Ess-peara," Max says as he puts the bed back and re-tucks the carpet. He opens the door.

"What's your name?" he asks.

"Margarita."

"Margarita, which is a great name by the way, I'm going to give you an extra five hundred pesos if you tell me what happened here."

"Pero señor, I—"

"I'm Rolando García with the DEA, and you can either help me or hold up my investigation."

Margarita stares at Max.

"DEA. ¿Comprende? Investigation. Muy importante."

"Only in Spanish."

"That's fine. I'll translate it later."

◎

At the hotel bar, Max struggles but manages to translate Margarita's words from his recorder:

> Well, I remember walking into the room in the morning to clean. No one answered when I knocked so I went in, and there he was. His blood everywhere. Everywhere. He looked at me, and I swear to you he exhaled his last breath. His soul must have been leaving his body. He waited to see that his body would be found, I think. What a terrible feeling, to not know if anyone will find your empty body.

Max becomes frustrated, reaching the point where drinking gin and tonics starts to hurt with each sip, his stomach's contents lapping like a wave pool. Yet, he orders another from the bartender with enough conviction to fool even himself. Max recalls coming home from that final talk with Magda, a memory as deep as a fatal wound. Then he savors another gin drink. Gin because it is the first hard booze he ever had. Max's then best friend snatched it out of his dad's liquor cabinet and said, "Nah, he won't notice." His dad never did notice, but the bartender places the gin and tonic in front of Max like exhibit A. Max finishes the drink, his phone vibrating in his pocket. The calling number is blocked, but Max answers it anyway.

"Someone's coming for you," a garbled voice says.

"Raúl?" Max asks. *He's the only person that's been given this number in Mexico*, Max remembers.

The call ends. Then, a beautiful woman parks herself at the bar-stool right next to Max.

"Hola," she says.

"Ho-la," Max responds.

"¡Ay! You speak Spanish very bad."

"That bad?"

"Yes. Very, very bad. You are lucky I speak English."

"And how'd you manage that?"

"Pues, it is very easy, no?"

"I suppose."

"No como el español. It is too much music for Americanos."

"Yes, but English is much more exact."

"¿Cómo? How?"

"We have several words that are alike yet more specific than others, whereas esspanole may only have a few."

"So? ¿Y qué?"

"It reaches at truth more, at something closest to the experience or meaning. Don't you think?"

"That is silly. La verdad no necesita ayuda. The truth does not need your help. You either say it, or not."

Max grins because he never thought of it like that. "I don't know. The truth takes a lot of digging to get to. It has to be right, and when you think you have it, you seize it."

She does not seem convinced.

"Pues," she says, while flicking her hair with whimsy, revealing a dark mole perfectly planted between her green eyes. "¿Qué bebes?"

"Gin and tonic. Ever had it?"

She shakes her head no.

"Here."

She takes a sip, and her face puckers before raising her hand to her mouth, giving back the drink. While her eyes are closed, Max looks straight into that third one. He feels magic radiate from her skin.

"¡Guacala! You have the taste of an old man."

"Yes, I'm afraid so," he laughs. Max gulps a quarter of his gin and tonic, shakily placing it down.

"You drink like a worried man, though. You are troubled."

"Yes, ma'am."

"What is your name?"

"Max."

"Max . . . ¿Como los Big Macs?"

"Ha. Yes, I suppose so."

"Max."

"Yours?"

"Yzobeau."

"Isabeau?"

"Yzobeau. Y-Z-O-B-E-A-U."

"Why the spelling?"

"I don't know. My mom wanted to make me unique, I guess."

"I get it. My name is actually Maximiliano."

"Ah. Much better than Big Macs."

"Perhaps, but it was either that or Vladimir. I suppose the Mexican in her won out."

"Well, Maximiliano."

"Please, call me Max."

"No. Max is ugly. Maximiliano is much better. Tiene algo . . . bravo."

"Sure," Max says. He then looks into his drink and wonders what fate or chance or calamity or what have you has appeared before him.

"It is a woman," Yzobeau says.

"What is?"

"That troubles you."

"How did you know?"

"It is always a woman. But this one, her name is Magda."

"How did you—," Max starts to ask.

"A secret," she says, "and I will tell you if you buy me a drink, Maximiliano."

"Name it."

"Whiskey and Coke."

Max tells the bartender immediately.

"Mi Lunar lets me see truths, into other dimensions."

"Is that so?"

"Sí. And in another dimension, you and Magda are very happy together."

"And what of reality?"

"Pues, it is real. Just not in this dimension. Never in this dimension," she says as her whiskey and Coke arrives. "You needed to hear that, no?"

Before the bartender leaves, Max asks for another gin and tonic.

"Maximiliano."

"Yeah?"

"Look at me," she commands. It takes a second, but Max works his eyes up from the bartop, up Yzobeau's arm, shoulder, neckline, cheek, lips, nose that leads perfectly into her forehead, and into her green eyes, avoiding direct contact with the mole. "Mira, I know what you're here for. I can help you. I know you only have thirty-eight hours to write the story."

Yzobeau places her hand on Max's. He can't help but look into Yzobeau's third eye. It is an aleph. Max sees into some other dimension where he and Yzobeau fall madly in love with each other. He witnesses all the moments where she stares at him and he at her, into each other's eyes in the intimacy of each other's warmth, and they believe right then and there, every time, that they love each other enough to believe that this is a world where every person has the winning lottery ticket and every child appreciates their mother and the stars and all the planets finally work in unison in that very moment to cast loneliness into the realm of laughable contemplations and afterthoughts, until the gorgeous heat death of the universe dissipates their bodies back into the primordial ether.

"What is this?" Max asks.

"Follow me," Yzobeau says and leads Max up to his room by the hand. Without his key, she opens the door and leaves the lights off.

Max and Yzobeau kiss; they begin slowly, and each kiss segues quickly into the next, just in time, lips locking down then up. She sits on the bed and takes off her dress, revealing her braless chest. She undoes Max's belt, dress pants falling to his brown oxfords. Max pushes her back onto the mattress.

What they don't teach you in school is that you have to work into some parts of the body. A slow and studious process, the trust that goes into it a wonder. And it's all pure abracadabra. She breathes through her mouth, like she's exercising. In, out. Deep breath and then exhale. She never looks back at Max, her eyes closed and head to the side, her long, curly hair spread on the sheets like a devouring void, as though she could disappear in an instant. Max goes slowly, her right hand on his belly to make sure he doesn't go any faster. Time passes.

Yzobeau pulls him in, her breathing the sound of a conch in his ear.

"Come inside me," she says.

He doesn't. Max backs off and sits on the mattress.

"What's wrong?"

"I-I don't know. I'm sorry."

"It's ok," Yzobeau whispers.

They sit there for a moment, just breathing. Not much else happens after that.

In fact, Max doesn't know when she leaves even though he never falls asleep. He simply turns onto his back and looks up to the ceiling, the moon dimly illuminating the white walls. He does nothing else. He thinks about what Yzobeau's third eye showed him but can't figure out why it wounds him so. Obviously, Max hasn't felt well since Magda left him, but Yzobeau made him feel infinitely happy for a moment, which she seemingly took with her as soon as she disappeared. Like a film strip, his memories of Magda play out on each of the walls of his hotel room, this memory in particular:

Max and Magda are in a car, post–movie date. It is their third date after first being introduced by a mutual college friend. They are silent and looking at everything but each other. The radio plays an Al Green song. Max notices their hands are near each other on the cup holders. Max finally puts his hand over hers. She flinches a little at first but looks down at their touching fingers before looking at him.

"Look, Magda. I make you so happy, you make me so happy. This can work. All I know is that if I lean in and give you a kiss, it'll be just right," Max says, turning his head to look out his window.

A woman's voice responds, "So, why don't you?"

Max turns around, and Yzobeau is looking right at him. She opens her mouth as though beginning to say something. A bright light crawls out of her third eye. He blinks.

Sunlight invades his hotel room, and the ocean hums as it always did. Max isn't sure if he slept or if what he remembers is just a dream from a sleep he doesn't recall.

"I'm fucking losing it," he says, getting up and running his fingers through his hair repeatedly. He has a little over twenty-four hours left to write the story. No real leads, a golden ring in his pocket, and nothing to send to his editor. He lays back down to try and sleep. It doesn't work.

◎

Max walks down to the hotel bar.

"Bloody Mary, por favor."

"We no open for other hour, señor."

"Just give me the drink," Max says, slipping a two-hundred-peso bill. "Mucho vodka, poor fayvor."

"Muy bien," the bartender replies.

"I'm Carlos, by the way. Carlos Carreón," Max says.

"Hello señor Carreón. Soy Martín."

"Marteen, tell me. Anything interesting happen around this place?"

"Claro, señor. There's always la playa, el mercado outside, and La Quebrada opens en la tarde."

"Los clabadeestas, right?"

"Yes, clavadistas, señor."

"What are they up to right now?"

"Preparando."

"Very good. Any chance I can see that? Talk to one of them? Just out of curiosity. I'm interested in how they don't crap their speedos before every jump."

"Sí, pero you have to be a special guest for that. Extra, extra dinero."

"I see. Only the shot callers, movers, and shakers, then?"

"Lo que sea. People with mucho dinero, sí."

Max figures that if he can speak to a clavadista, he can get a lead on who still spends big money in the hotel, maybe even the person who sells around here. He knocks back his Bloody Mary, the sharpness of the vodka and hot sauce burning his throat and nostrils. He winces, pseudo salutes the bartender, and leaves the hotel to head to La Quebrada. He notices there is a guard booth that stops patrons to make them pay for entry. Max walks over to a nearby bodega and buys a twelve-pack of beer and a bag of limes. He heads back to La Quebrada, and rather than going through the guard booth, goes straight toward a nearby bungalow where the hunched janitor sweeps.

"Ho-la. ¿Cómo 'stá?" Max asks.

"Lo siento, señor. Please go to tourist information. Sorry, sorry."

"I know where I am. Wondering if you could do me a favor."

"No, sorry, sorry. Please go."

"I got you." Max flashes a two-hundred-peso bill. "Nes-ses-seeto hablar con un clabadeesta."

"I speak inglés, señor."

"Yeah, I need to talk to a cliff diver."

Max hands over the 200-peso bill.

"I don't know, señor."

Max flashes another two-hundred-peso bill, nudging at the twelve-pack at his feet.

"My name's Pedro, and I need to talk to a cliff diver. I'm writing a book, and they won't let me talk to the cliff divers because I can't afford the special package. You understand, right?"

"¿Un libro?"

"Yeah, leebro. What's your name?"

"Ohtli."

"Ohtli, it's easy. You keep the four hundred pesos. You just take me to a cliff diver, talk for ten minutes, and I'm out. Hell, if you translate for me, I'll throw in another two hundred pesos."

"¿Seiscientos pesos?"

"Sounds nice, right? Even drink some beers. Ten minutes."

"Sí, ten minutes."

"All I need. I'm making art. You're helping an artist."

"Sí, como poesía."

"Right? I got ya. Neruda? Paz?"

"Me encanta Octavio Paz."

"There you go. I'm trying to be Paz is all."

"Sí, I help you."

"You're a good man, Ohtli. Good man."

Ohtli leads Max down a small path alongside the cliff, the waves crashing beneath them. They walk until they reach an area where the clavadistas climb back up from the ocean, wet and shiny.

"Look, señor."

Ohtli points upward to a clavadista stepping to the edge of a cliff, arms spread open to accept the sea wind. He looks down at the water scratching thunderously at the black rocks of the mountain he stands on, brings his hands together in prayer, and leaps, his arms now behind him like a newborn chick's wings. Perhaps it is the ocean mist blurring Max's vision or the skyward pull of the invisible moon, but the clavadista seems to fall at the same speed throughout his dive, as consistent as the planets must travel around the sun in their predestined treading. The clavadista plunges into the black ocean, the foaming surface undisturbed by such minutiae. He does not resurface for several seconds. When his head breaks the turbulent surface, he inhales deeply through his nose and exhales through his tightened lips. He slowly paddles to the platform Max and Ohtli stand on and lifts his drenched body to his feet.

"That was amazing," Max whispers.

"Dice que fue maravilloso," Ohtli translates.

"Gracias, amigo," the clavadista says.

"Do you have a moment to talk?"

"¿Tienes un momento para hablar, Manuel?"

"Pos sí," the clavadista states, smoothing his black hair.

"He say yes."

"Very good."

Manuel leads Ohtli and Max to a nearby shack. Manuel goes into it and puts on a white t-shirt and tire-soled sandals and comes out holding a small box in his right hand. Outside, the three men sit at a white table with a blue umbrella and four plastic chairs.

"¿Qué onda?" asks Manuel.

"Lo mismo, como siempre Manuel. Él es un escritor, quiere hablar contigo para su libro."

"Muy bien. My name is Manuel. I don't know much inglés. I will speak in Spanish."

"That's fine. My name is Pedro," Max says. "Ohtli here can translate."

"Voy a traducir por este pocho."

"Oye bien, Pedro. Así se llamaba mi padre."

"He say his father's name is Pedro."

"That's awesome." Max pulls a notepad out of his back pocket and lifts three beers to the table. "Poor fayvor, gentlemen. Help yourselves."

"Nos trajo cerveza."

"Que amable. Thank you, Pedro. Salud."

They clink their brown bottles together and gulp a neck's worth of beer.

"Tell me, Manuel, how did you come to jump off cliffs for a living?"

"¿Cómo te hiciste clavadista?"

"Es lo que hacía mi padre. Me enseñó desde que tenía once años."

"His father was clavadista. He teach Manuel since eleven."

"Great. How'd your father get into this?"

"¿Cómo tu padre se hizo clavadista?"

"Pues mi abuelo también."

"His grandfather, too."

"How are they now?"

"¿Cómo están?"

"Muertos, los dos."

"Dead."

"How?"

"¿Cómo?"

"Mi abuelo era alcohólico. Murió joven. Mi padre saltó en el mal momento y pegó las piedras. Se rieron los delfines."

"He say his grandfather was alcoholic, die young. His father jump in the bad moment and hit the rocks. The dolphins laughed."

"When did that happen?"

"¿Cuándo sicedió?"

"La semana antes de mi primer salto en frente las turistas. El murió en frente de los gringos y ellos tomaron fotos."

"One week before Manuel start jumping in front of tourists. His father die in front of tourists, and they take pictures."

"I'm sorry, Manuel," Max says, noticing the thin film of tears enveloping Manuel's eyeballs. The ocean roars in the distance.

"Lo siente."

"Thank you, Pedro. Yo ayude sacar el cuerpo de mi padre del mar. Recuerdo que su cuerpo fue tan débil en el agua, sus brazos y piernas flojos con el corriente. Pero cuando lo levanté a las piedras, sentí cuanto peso tenía cada músculo en su cuerpo. Mi padre fue fuerte y se ocuparón todas las piedras de esta montaña para matarlo."

"He took his father's body from out the ocean. His father's body weak in the water. His arms and legs go with the current. He lifted his father's body onto the rocks. He said his father so strong, it took all the rocks of the mountain to kill him."

"Why did you still become a clavadista, then?"

"¿Porque seguiste ser clavadista, pues?"

"Espera." Manuel raises his hand up to pause everything.

Manuel then snatches another beer from the box and chugs it. He puts the small box he has with him on the tabletop and opens it. Manuel pulls a small pouch of white powder out and sets up lines of cocaine, which he promptly snorts. The tears in his eyes drag down his face. He snaps his head back and rubs his face with his palms. Manuel stays in this position, staring up into the cloudless sky. He drums his fingers on the armrests of his chair to no particular beat.

"Ese día mismo, más temprano, mi padre y yo comimos juntos en un restaurante cerca de aquí. Hablamos sobre la vida, sobre una mujer con quien me quería casar. Pues, nada pasó con ella, pero tú sabes cómo es la vida. Yo comí chilaquiles y él comió huevos rancheros. Cuando acabamos, fuimos afuera a fumar y mi padre apuntó a las piedras abajo. Allí, sobre una piedra blanca, había tres gatitos dormidos juntos. Aparecieron como órganos peludos pegados para calentarse, la piedra vibrando con olas infinitas para cantarnos antes de dormir. Desde ese momento, yo entendí porque yo quería ser clavadista como mi padre. Y si esos gatitos no tuvieron miedo al mar, yo tampoco. El mar hace mucho ruido, pero no dice nada nuevo. Mi padre me enseñó eso. Perdón. ¿Ustedes quieren un poco?"

Manuel offers some cocaine to Ohtli and Max. They both pass.

"He say that—"

"Yeah, yeah, yeah. I got it. Where'd he get the cocaine?" Max asks.

"What?"

"Where'd he get the cocaine?"

"¿Dónde conseguiste la cocaína?"

"Tú sabes, de esos hombres en los trajes blancos."

"From men in white suits who come sometimes to the hotel."

"White suits? Where are they?"

"They are not here all the time. They only come sometimes."

"Do you know anyone else they make contact with? Anyone who can lead me to them?"

"¿Sabes cómo encontrar a esos hombres?"

Manuel looks out into the sea, quivering and holding back tears. "Ya sabes. Esa mujer. La bruja."

"Chingada madre. He say there is a woman who comes with them a lot."

"A woman? Does she have a mole? Between her eyes?"

"Sí, ella."

Max hides his excitement, knowing he must confront Yzobeau again with a lead in mind.

"Very good. Thank you. This all really helped my book. Manuel, how you doing over there?"

Manuel sits there, motionless, save for some muscle twitches and hiccups. However, the hoarse sea is interrupted by the laughter of dolphins gathering in the gulch, four or five of them swarming underneath the surface. Manuel immediately stands up and yells at them, throwing one of his sandals and stringing curse words together without stopping for breath. Ohtli runs over to try and console him. Max leaves, unsure what to say or do for Manuel because, sometimes, a person's sadness is so pelagic that others become lost in contemplating its depth.

Max rushes back to the hotel, calculating that he has about sixteen hours left to write the story, a golden ring in his pocket, and one lead to tie them together.

◎

Maximiliano Mondragón sits at the Hotel Agua Clara bar and waits for Yzobeau, the woman who haunts his memories and holds the real answers to his real questions. To pass the time, he writes down Magda's name over and over again until it becomes Yzobeau, drinking beer, gin, a margarita, more beer, more gin, another margarita, until he reaches a desired state of drowsiness that he misinterprets as peace. The sounds of other people's voices are muffled. But the sea's not-too-far-off moaning still places a haze over his brain that he finds endearing because time is always inexact when you attempt to decipher what the ocean is harping on about.

"Hello, Max."

"Yzobeau, funny seeing you here."

"Always the charmer, sí? Been waiting for me? Not too long, I hope."

"Whiskey and Coke?"

"Ay, and ever gracious."

"Whiskey and Coke for the lady."

"How's your day, Maximiliano?"

"Ok. Really ok. Then you showed up. Now, it's perfect."

"¿Y el artículo? Is Rep. de Luz giving you a hard time from beyond the grave?"

"I've got a lead. It's you."

"¡Mira! ¿Yo? You start too many conversations and the next thing you know, a murder is on your hands."

"Please, tell me who did it."

"There's reality, and there's the story you are writing. Pick one."

"Who killed de Luz?" Max grabs Yzobeau's wrist and holds it tight.

"You're drunk, Maximiliano. I liked you better as a worried man."

"I don't know what that third eye is doing to me, but it's got me all fucked up. The least you can do is answer my question."

"La verdad, the truth, isn't always what's best. You can leave, and we can have what happened stay as it is. Or you can see what's going on."

"Show me, Yzobeau. I'll stay right here until you do."

"Ay, Maximiliano . . ." Yzobeau laments. She acquiesces because this could either be the next part in a sequence of events that leads to Aceves's end or another dead end. The risk is more than worth it, she figures.

Yzobeau parts her hair from her forehead and leans into Max, the Lunar waiting to be seen. Max focuses on the peephole to look into the past. He sees the murderer, the murder itself, how a man dug his thumb into Rep. de Luz's eye socket and another man nearby laughed, how the man in a white suit took a knife from his boot and drove it into Rep. de Luz's throat, Rep. de Luz clawing at the man's torso, gurgling to stop but he knew it was too late. Max also witnesses different portions of different lives but can't remember any after he sees them, left with lingering senses of emotion or images without their context, like dreams or a television speeding through channels. He remembers three things: (1) Every person has the same, tired face in all of them; (2) the dead awake from their sleep to consume the living; and (3) a city sprouts from dirt and screams with light until night picks off each illumination like coins over the eyes.

Max even experiences his own demise in an abstract sense, noting that he dies alone but not afraid. It is the opposite of his birth, where he is weeping and confused, and the specter of creation is latching onto his heels. *So many civilizations had it figured out for us,*

Max. Yet here we are, up to the same old shit. Max, there are stories and there's the Truth. You can't do anything with the truth because it won't change anything here or now or ever.

The only other person to experience a sentiment this profound is Yzobeau. Swollen with mezcal, beer, marijuana, LSD, and cocaine at a party, she stumbles into the restroom and grabs the edges of a sink as though she is on a rocking ship. The cocktail of porquerías in her system makes reality into an off-sync video where the audio is either ahead or behind the footage, where an image she is experiencing in the present already came and went, with whatever happening in between lost. Though she knows not to look up into the mirror and at her Lunar, she already did seconds ago. Where her head should be, there's a kaleidoscope of gold teeth, turquoise feathers, shards of stained glass, and green moss that is interrupted with flashes of other realities.

One moment, she is an angler fish near the bottom of an ocean fusing with another angler fish, their organs melding into one anatomy. Another moment, she sees Gabriel sit on the floor and try to keep his organs in his belly from spilling out, a headless man standing above him, gripping a shard of pure light in his hand. Otra, she is a bear chasing a helicopter to huff the trail of engine leakage dampening the snow. Otra, Yzobeau sees herself escaping another city consumed by smoke in a golden truck with her sister, mother, and father. In another, she is a tardigrade watching the surface of the earth curdle like meat in a petri dish.

When she regains bearing in this reality, the thought of finding the man who will lead to El Gacho's demise sobers her into an obsession. *Be careful Yzobeau. Just because two people experience something together doesn't mean it's meant to be.* Though her curse is to defeat El Gacho, Max may or may not be a link in this chain of history. Only time will tell.

"I can take you to see the men you are looking for," Yzobeau interrupts, snapping Max back into this reality.

"What?"

"Did you see the murder?"

"Yes."

"What else did you see?"

"N-nothing. Yeah, that'd be great."

"Maximiliano, what else did you see?"

"Never mind. It's all good. Take me to them."

Max wonders if any of this means anything. There are fourteen hours until his deadline.

◎

Maximiliano Mondragón and Yzobeau take a cab. They go along la playa, and Max sees all the glitzy bars passing him by, lights upon lights flashing in every color from our earthly spectrum. The music is so loud that the sea mist trembles in the moonlight. However, the lights from the clubs do not illuminate the night sky that fuses with the rum-colored ocean. In the distance are tiny white eyes. Max and Yzobeau arrive at a club, one that overlooks Acapulco. Max is stopped and frisked. Yzobeau is welcomed and kissed on the cheek by the bouncer.

The club's interior shifts every half second with chromatic colors of blue, green, red, yellow, and white, causing women with man-crushing curves and drunk men who are dancing to look as though they are rapidly passing images from a slide projector. Yzobeau navigates the crowd and leads Max down a short hall to a lounge area where the music is just vibrations. She kisses Max on the cheek and points to two gentlemen wearing white suits sitting in a booth. One man is considerably smaller than the other. Yzobeau sits down in another booth alone, takes out a cigarette, and crosses her legs. The shorter of the two gentlemen smiles and calls Max over.

"Hola," he says.

"Ho-la."

"English it is."

"How does everyone know English?"

"Well, for me, my best customers speak English."

"What do you sell?"

"I think you know what I do."

"I'd rather you tell me."

"I help smuggle drugs, people, guns, all the shit Americans love, jefe. I also deal with loose ends, as I'm sure you've seen."

Max remembers he is the man laughing in the vision, wearing a similar white suit with a white, buttoned-up shirt, no tie. Though he is wearing sunglasses. The other man in the booth is also wearing a white suit, but is immense, built like a statue of some god or warrior and staring at nothing in particular.

"Don't mind him. El Chango is as harmless as I tell him to be."

"What's his name?"

"El Chango. You've seen his handiwork."

"What's your name?"

"Gabriel. But call me El Gacho."

"Gotcho?"

"Close enough."

"Sorry."

"No, no. It's ok. It's just a nickname, and the best nicknames are the ones you earn."

"I suppose."

"¿Pues?"

"Oh, I'm Jack."

"*Jack*. Qué nombre fuerte. *Jack*," El Gacho repeats, swelling up his chest and puffing his cheeks.

"Very funny."

"Yes. Anyways, down to business, Mr. Jack."

"Which is?"

"I know why you're here. And let me just say that de Luz deserved everything he had done to him."

"Why is that?"

"The man sold out to the highest bidder."

"So it's true."

"Yes, your elected official was corrupt and in turn corrupted your beloved city."

"I see."

"Yes, yes. It appears you Americans are more corrupt than you perceive the Mexicans to be."

"What did he give you?"

"Cooperation."

"How deep does it go?"

"Let's say that district, that ship channel, everything in it, belongs to me."

"Why did you kill him, then?"

"De Luz became a real boy. Too late though, much too late. And when boys try to be men, you have to teach them. El Chango here prefers his teaching to be hands on. Right, Chango?"

El Chango snorts a line of cocaine and hangs his gargantuan head back, giggling through his teeth.

"Oh, Chango. Míralo."

"Why are you telling me all this?"

"I'm a proud one, Jack. What good is it to be the best if the world does not know it?"

"You do know that me publishing this story will result in things only getting harder for you both here and in Houston?"

"Yes, but you make it sound so easy. Mr. Jack, this information is not free. No, if you publish this, I will make sure El Chango here visits you in Houston."

"Why did you even bother telling me all this, then?"

"Because now comes the best part. I am not so simple, Jack. By telling you this, the responsibility is on you now. Will you be a good man and tell the world at the cost of your life? Or will you be a de Luz and die like a coward, never telling the truth? What are you going to choose?"

"I've been in this business a while, Gacho. That's the craziest fucking thing I've heard. Is this all a game to you?"

"Yes!" El Gacho exclaims. "That's all I'm here for, Jack. To complicate things."

"I see that. I'll have you know, I'm not afraid to die these days."

Max and El Gacho lock eyes and neither blinks. El Gacho breaks eye contact to serve himself a shot of clear liquid that he gulps. He doesn't wipe the wet from his lips.

"Is that so? Well, every man has his limits, Jack," El Gacho says.

"You're a man too, Gabriel."

El Gacho stands up and knocks the table over in the booth.

"You are wearing out my patience, Mondragón. Mistaken on two accounts. One, El Chango and I are not men. Two, you are afraid of death. Perhaps not of yours, but afraid of death nonetheless."

El Chango puts his palms to his forehead, rocks front to back, and mutters, "Quiero matar, quiero matar, quiero matar."

"You think we don't know of Magda?"

Max's face does not change.

"Bien duro este. ¿Eh, Chango?"

"Quiero matar, Gacho. Quiero matar. Déjame matar."

"Mondragón," El Gacho says, raising his hand and pointing his index finger to Max's face. He steps back to throw a bottle on the table against a wall, shattering it into pieces. El Gacho snaps his fingers at Yzobeau before lifting his hand to smooth over his hair.

"Some mezcal, mi bellísima," El Gacho orders with a smile.

Yzobeau comes with a bottle and two glasses and pours each of them drinks. She looks at Max, concerned. Max is reminded that he is in love with her. El Gacho grabs Yzobeau by the hips and pulls her onto his lap.

"Gracias, bella. Beautiful, ah, Mondragón? Took quite the few Indians and Spaniards to fuck and get this mixture just right."

"I guess. Sure."

"You are a fool, Mondragón."

"How's that, Gacho?"

"Only fools fall in love with what they cannot have."

Max breathes in through his nose.

"Ahí está. I knew it. You love her," El Gacho says, sipping his mezcal. "She belongs to me, you know."

Max refuses to respond. Yzobeau turns to El Gacho. He snaps his head back to avoid contact with her mole.

"No me mires, puta."

El Gacho seizes Yzobeau's chin and forces her to look at Max. Max looks away. He is too afraid.

"Chango, make him see," El Gacho commands.

El Chango lifts his giant body from his seat and walks over to Max so fast that Max didn't realize when El Chango placed his mitt-sized hands around his skull. El Chango turns Max's head to face the mole, and he is so strong that Max feels like a child in his struggle to fight back.

"This Lunar of hers, it makes you see crazy things, si? I don't like it. El Chango loved looking into it and look at him now," El Gacho says.

Max opens his eyes and looks upward at El Chango who is mesmerized by images of: someone's stomach being split open with roses spilling out; a gun drooling cum from its barrel; a sky raining knives.

"What's wrong, Mondragón? Don't you feel like a hero?" El Gacho mocks. "Ya sabes, Mondragón, that I like to play with my toys? In fact, I can put El Chango and Yzobeau into a room together. You see, El Chango mixes up his knife and his dick sometimes. Chiiin, why not get you in there? El Chango doesn't mind. ¿Verdad, Chango?"

El Chango doesn't respond, still entranced.

"¡Ya párale!" El Gacho yells. El Chango blinks, shakes his head, and releases Max. He then walks over to his seat and sits with his hands on his knees.

"Please, Gacho. Just let her go. You win. I'm just some asshole in over his head, okay? Let her go."

El Gacho pushes Yzobeau off his lap.

"Are we done here, Gacho?" Yzobeau asks.

"Cuando me de la chingada gana."

"You've said what you wanted to say, querido. Por favor. You've bested him. What else do you want?"

"Pues. Yes, fine. Take him back y te veo mañana," El Gacho says. "If I see you again, Americano . . . híjole . . ."

Max gets up to leave.

"Espera. The ring. Take good care of it. I don't know how you journalists work, but I'm sure it'll be good proof, no? It's de Luz's. Make you look more credible with all this absurdity going on. Unless you think the finger will be better?" El Gacho laughs at his own joke.

Max digs into his pocket and finds that it is still there.

"No, it's fine."

El Chango spins the tip of a large knife on his thigh like a ballerina, driving the tip so that blood begins to trickle onto his white pants.

"Remember Mondragón: the truth shall set you free!"

When Max leaves the club, he curses his life, the Truth, the music that spills out into the streets, the mathematical probability of the moment that has just occurred, that every choice he ever made in his life perfectly culminating at such a fine-tuned point.

"Are you okay?" Yzobeau asks.

"Just dandy."

"It's all a game to him, Maximiliano. It'll be his downfall. You have to believe that."

They hail a taxi and climb inside. They both look out their window for a while. Yzobeau is the first to break the silence.

"Are you going to write the story?"

"I-I don't know, Yzobeau."

"You must!"

"Didn't you fucking hear that lunatic? What he'll do to you?"

"Yes, I did. I can take care of myself. But someone has to stop him. We can. You saw him. He doesn't even share this reality with us. The story will piss off the wrong people who can kill him. I see that now."

"How can you be so sure that that's what happens in this reality?"

"It's the only lead we have. Look at what he's doing to this city. To your city. To me. You're here for a reason, Maximiliano."

"Just give me a second to think."

Max looks outside the taxi window, the shimmering sea and the city lights indistinguishable from each other. He has six hours.

◎

Max and Yzobeau return to the Hotel Agua Clara bar. He orders a gin and tonic, she a whiskey and Coke.

"Maximiliano, I—"

"Yzobeau, I'm in love with you. Sick in love with you. And when you tell me we're never going to be together, I'm going to keep being sick. For a long time."

"The more reason to write the story, amor. If you love me, you'll write it."

Yzobeau covers her mole with her hair and looks into her drink. "In another dimension, you and I are very happy together. The only thing I cannot see is if our child is a boy or a girl."

"And what of reality?"

"Pues, it is real. Just not in this dimension." Yzobeau puts her finger in her drink and swirls the liquid.

Yzobeau believes Maximiliano is in love with her. She really does. But that's never been the point. Love is simply another means to an end. Yzobeau has seen her life conclude in so many ways, but the one that stood out to her was dying in a bed from old age with people crying around her. This could be the reality wherein which this occurs, but Yzobeau knows its fulfillment isn't possible with Gacho alive. Maximiliano could be anything, but most of all, he can be El Gacho's death. Yzobeau recalls a reality where she visits a giant tortoise who raises its head to return her stare; its obsidian eyes flicker with sunlight before softening into velvet.

Maximiliano Mondragón feels the golden ring pulse in his pocket and wonders if there exists a dimension where he makes the right choice. He has four hours to turn in something to his editor. He looks over at the clavadistas diving into the black ocean from 115 feet in the air. He envies them.

LILIA

FEMALE. 8 YEARS OLD. 3'5". Hazel eyes she got from her mother that burned like rusty flames around a black sun. Coca-Cola black hair that in sunlight glowed cherubic gold. Puffy cheeks with lips between them that opened to reveal Chiclet-white teeth whenever she was cooed to sleep.

Died in the back seat of this reddish car. Coughs scraped out of her little larynx like a knife over toast, before less oxygen went into her lungs than out, before the whistly wheezing became airless choking, before the grip she had on my hand became the soft scratching into my palm, before I looked back at her as we pulled into the hospital parking lot and never seeing her again. This was before I went kind of crazy, before I did and said a bunch of stupid shit, before I lost my job and her mother, and before I begged everyone not to leave. It didn't work.

I'm not going to go too much into detail of what my life was before Lilia, or after, because none of it is of any use anymore. Let's just say driving people from point A to point B in this car is all I'm good for now. It happens. Anyways, it's my overnight shift I took on after not making enough during daylight hours last month, bills piling up near the front door like hourglass sand.

I start as the sun finishes setting, what's left of its purple residue still lingering over the Houston skyline. I clean the interior of my car by vacuuming the seats and picking up anything left from passengers. Sometimes, I'll find a long strand of hair that I hold up to a light. I always examine them closely, and they all glow with the same yellow so I'm never sure how long it's been since Lilia . . . I then let the strand of hair go to be devoured by the damp ether until it returns to my car. I accept this as simply another process of the universe so that the earth remains on its axis.

I then log into the vehicle-for-hire service on my phone and wait for someone to request a ride. Their name and destination will show up, and I hope for the ones that require me to go around downtown. I like driving near the skyscrapers on 45, their yellow lights fading in and out across my skin and dashboard as I pass them. It reminds me of a time when I was a citizen of the world.

And there they are: Madison. Female. 25-27 years old. White. Short, blonde hair. From Downtown to Golfcrest. Odd.

I put the keys in the ignition, turn my wrist until the car takes its first deep breath of the night, and drive. From there, I merge on the feeder to get onto the freeway, the connecting ramp closing in, in 1-2-3. There it is. Every ramp has a shift in the consistency of the asphalt when the tar road meets the concrete freeway. When a tire drives over this line, there's a muffled clicking sound you can feel and hear that reverberates into the hollow space of the overpass, each time slightly different, as it varies on how many homeless lie asleep, or how bad traffic is, or how sweltering thick the air rests, carrying sound with the consistency of molasses.

Though Houston shifts and changes constantly, what doesn't change is that everything is where it always has been: the poor here, the rich there, Black and Brown people más allá, the white ones over yonder. Anything not belonging to those categories merely attempts to hide this paradigm. The same could be said of any city.

The same could be said of America. The same could be said of the world. So, when Madison wants me to pick her up from somewhere downtown and probably take her home, I already know a few things about her: she has energy to burn, and she's afraid of loneliness. A deadly combination. I should know. The heavy lights of the city splash on my skin, and it feels right.

I pull up to a bougie-ass restaurant where only appetizers and cocktails are served. There are four people outside, two of them holding up someone in a short, blue dress. Female. 23 to 25 years old. Long, black hair. Latina. It all makes sense now. Another young woman, white, approaches my car.

"Are you Madison?" I ask.

"Yeah, but the ride is for my friend here," she says as the others dump that woman in my back seat. "She's had a bit too much to drink."

Usually, I'd object, but the fare is too good to pass up. Out of twenty-three rides needed in the area, this one is mine.

"What's her name?"

"Thanks so much!" Madison says as she drunk stomps back into a bar's façade.

"Hey, you alright back there?" I ask.

No answer. That's fine. I turn on the radio because too much silence allows for thoughts to go where they shouldn't. I always try different stations every night so as to surprise my mind. This time, it's a classic rock station with a right-wing DJ at the helm.

". . . those Democraps are ruining this country. I pray to God every day to make our country right again, strong again. Dang shame. Anyways, the count is now 6 years, 150 days, 12 hours, 26 minutes, since that village in Kenya started missing its idiot. Now, here's the Eagles with 'Take it Easy.'"

"Hey, can you change this shit?" the young woman asks. "I don't want to listen to this racist asshole. Or the fucking Eagles."

"Fair enough."

I change the station.

"¡Aquí estamos en el Cloob Bandidos donde las mujeres entran gratis y los hombres pagan todo! ¡Ven y ponte pedo, hyperrrrr, sexy-issimo con DJ Cabeza de Chocha!" The broadcast sounds like it's on location, the cumbia tribal music scratchy with the heavy bass and drunken dancers wooing as the DJ yells away from the mic, "Dale y dale, así, así . . ."

"Where am I, by the way?" the girl in the backseat moans.

"You're in a vehicle for hire. Taking you home."

"No, I'm with my friends." She starts to feel out her surroundings, the leather warping with her every move.

"Madison asked me to take you home. Sit still, and we'll be there in no time."

"Take me back to Madison. It's her birthday, and she's my BFF."

"It's probably better if you go home."

She panics, reaching over and trying to force the car door open, not realizing the door is locked, then hitting the window with her palm.

"Look! Madison ordered a ride to take you home. It didn't seem like they wanted you there, alright?"

Sometimes we have to save people from themselves. It happens. She lies back down. I drive for a while. It's all going pretty smoothly, until we get into her subdivision. And shit, there it fucking is. A train. The arms of its crossing signal lower, and the bell screams. Fuck.

"Hey, the train's coming. Know any way around?" I ask the young woman.

"Nope! We have to wait it out. Fucking Houston, huh?"

"Fucking Houston."

I turn up the radio:

"Aquí estamos en Cloob Bandidos con bebidas fuertes y mujeres pretty-íssimas! ¿Verdad chicas? ¿Pues qué haces? ¡Ven a Cloo-cloo-cloob Bandidos-dos con DJ Cabeza-beza de Chocha-chocha-chocha!"

"I haven't been to that one," the girl in the backseat says.

"No? You like that kind of stuff?"

"Totes. I think once I get a chance to dance with him, things will change. I like him. Like a lot."

I look in the rearview mirror and see her drawing designs in the air with the twinkling of her fingers, loops and lines as though conducting a spell.

"He like you back?" I ask to pass the time.

"I don't know. I don't know, Idunno. Idunno."

"I'm sorry," I say. I don't mean it. It's just something I've learned to say in moments of other people's sadness.

"Yeah. Ok." I can hear her shift to her side, now facing the leather cushions.

"¡Está es una bueníssimaaaaa fiesta!" the DJ sings.

"It's best to not think about what he's doing right now," I say. It's true. I did it all the time with my ex-wife, and all I got was a few scars on my knuckles.

But it's too late. She starts to heave, then whimpers. If I don't intervene, the whimpers will become full blown weeping, then coughs, then a decision has to be made. I should know.

"Listen to me," I say. "What's your name?"

The young woman struggles to sit up, squirming in her tight dress like a toppled penguin.

"Layla," she says, running her hands through her hair.

"Layla what?"

"Velarill."

"Velarill? Wait, you mean Villarreal?"

"Yeah, but that's not how I say it."

"Okay. Layla. So, tell me," I begin. "When was the last time you were happy?"

"Me?"

"No, the other passenger."

Layla looks around.

"You're funny," she says. "What's the happiest day of my life? I'll tell mine if you tell yours. Deal?"

"Sure," I say. Hopefully, this train passes soon, and we get there before she finishes.

"Ummmmm, ok. I guess it would have to be when I first met my father."

"Met your father? Like, formally?"

"Yeah. I was raised by my grandma. When my dad got custody again, my grandma dropped me off at his job at the end of his shift. I remember waiting there for him, so excited. The restaurant he worked at had this huge neon sign that was so bright that I couldn't see what it said. I saw this dark figure come out, and my grandma said it was him. I stepped out of the car and stood there, waiting for him to come closer. He was so tall, or maybe I was so little. But when he got closer, the huge light got smaller and smaller. Until he got close enough for me to hug him. It was like it was meant to happen that way, like he came out of heaven." The train keeps going. Its bellowing shakes the moon.

"Wow," I say.

"Right? Yeah. It's been pretty great ever since," she says with runny makeup. "You?"

"Me?"

"Yeah you, fool. What's the happiest day of your life?"

I pause because I'm making up a story. I can't tell her the happiest day of my life, nothing even close to it. How about this: I'll tell her the opposite of the worst day of my life. No, fool, the opposite of the worst day is not always the happiest day. In fact, the opposite of my worst day is what should've been the happiest day. While you only get one happiest day of your life, you get many what-should-have-beens. The imagination is one-half cruelty, one-half hope. The inhale, the exhale. I'm doing this because every person deserves that story they keep to themselves lest they tell every story they know. They won't have anything new to give to the world. Then what good are you? The train seems infinite.

Here it goes:

"It was my um wedding day. Me and my bride, her name is uh Lisa, we had been dating for uh five years actually. Vanilla wedding cake, friends, family. All that stuff. Yeah. That's pretty much it."

"That's it?" she asks.

"What do you mean?"

"You're lying. I know you are. You're a bad liar. I can tell."

"How do you figure that?" That story wasn't a complete lie, but I suppose half of a lie is still a lie.

"You've spoken with certainty this whole time, until that story. You were making it up as you went. I can tell."

She's smarter than I thought. Either way, she can take it or leave it. It's my car.

"Why do you care?" I ask.

"Because you asked me a question. I answered it truthfully, and you're giving me bullshit. If you don't want to talk to me, then fucking don't. I hate liars."

Layla then sits up and pulls out her phone. She's right. I'm a liar. I can see why her friends are sending her home. No one likes the truth. People send the truth away in bottles in the ocean, not to be found but to have hope in their situation. I don't like being that person, a liar. Billboards and signs and people lie out there to get you to love them or give them money or vote for them. To lie is to celebrate them. I don't want to be a liar. Not to someone who, in some other life, may have been my daughter.

"Lilia—I mean Layla, I'm sorry."

She says nothing.

"Layla, did you hear me? I'm sorry."

She continues to ignore me. Perhaps she is my daughter. Some religions believe that souls exit the body and inhabit another. Others believe everything is part of some divine plan. I don't believe in any of those. But the only thing I can do in this life is to hold my own soul accountable to myself. If not, then who am I? Perhaps telling the truth is the only way to make certain your soul doesn't disappear.

"Layla, I'm going to tell you the truth. The happiest day of my life is the day my daughter was born."

She remains silent.

"The happiest day of my life was every day with my daughter, really. That's the truth."

"The truth, sure. But not the Truth, capital T. I gave you a specific day and what happened. That was the deal. Happiest *day* of your life. Come on."

"Damn. You're right. Let's see . . . Ok. Here it is. One day, I took my daughter to la pulga. You know what those are, right?"

"Sí, asshole."

"Anyways, I took her to la pulga, the one where I grew up going to as a kid. And we go, and I show her all my favorite spots, like to get licuados, the rides, look at all those knock-off toys. All that good shit. We end up buying a puppy. We were going to raise it together, like a daughter-father sorta project. You know?"

"Yeah. That's cute."

"I could see the light in her eyes become especially bright, you know, the kind of light you see when you give your child something that'll last. Like a car or a blessing to marry someone or whatever. You know?"

"For sure. I didn't think about it like that. From a dad's perspective, I mean."

"Y'all never do. It's something you won't know until you do it. Have a kid, you know?"

"What happened? You said it in a past tense way. 'Were going to raise it together,' you said. Future in the past tense, as in it was true but no longer."

"Shit. You an English major or something?"

"Sure. What happened to the puppy?"

"I don't remember, to tell you the truth."

"What? Did it die or run away or something?"

"I told you. I don't remember."

That's the truth. The dog may be with my ex-wife. I don't know. I don't know.

"Well, does your daughter know that the dog is missing?"

"No. She doesn't."

"When are you going to tell her? If that's the happiest day of your life, that dog's gotta be really important to you two. Is she off at college or . . . ?"

"No. She's not off at college."

"Well . . . I think you should tell her. That's a pretty important thing to not tell her. It was a promise y'all made!"

"You're right. I wish I could tell her."

"Why can't you?"

"¡Vengan, vengan, vengan! ¡Y olviden sus chones!" DJ Cabeza de Chocha invites the world. I turn off the radio because here it comes. The Truth. Capital T.

"She's dead, Layla. My daughter's dead." Layla doesn't say anything. The pause is too long. I'd say something else, but the Truth is out. There's nothing left to say. The train finishes passing, as though on cue. The arms raise. I drive. I peek in the rearview mirror, and Layla looks out the window. There's nothing to see, really. Just houses and lawns and fences shrouded in night. Maybe that's everything.

I pull up to an apartment complex entrance, to where the GPS tells me.

"Here you are. Good luck with everything, Layla." I mean it.

"Thank you. If I could give you four out of five stars, I would," Layla says. Fair enough.

She then gets out of the car and out of my life. That's the only Truth. People come and go. Some sooner than others. Some better than others. I complete some other rides, and I don't talk to any of them. What's the point? How many times must one repeat the Truth? I'm not sure, actually. I might need to say it more and more. Until it becomes everyone's Truth, maybe. I stop taking riders. I get on the interstate to get home. The lights turn my skin into the color of heaven.

I get off the interstate, and that bump happens, notes to a song I can't understand yet. Once you get deeper into the streets and coast along, a smorgasbord of lights stabs your eyes. Houston's built like a puzzle crammed together from different boxes, too far in to quit but not quite finished either. There could be a shanty burger joint in your vision one second, a Romanesque strip joint with columns and a billboard the next; a bright red tax office begs for your attention in a strip mall while a massage parlor obscured by tinted windows patiently stands alongside a nail salon that still has the open sign on. A theater from the '50s could now be a Mexican restaurant or a grocery store. A basketball stadium becomes a megachurch. We Houstonians don't like to get bored so we're animals of whim, cursed to always wander but blessed to love every second of it. This nature ingrains a forgetfulness in every Houstonian. We love to forget, but I can't. That's a blessing and a curse. It happens. To remember things in Houston is to become its enemy and its favorite child. I suppose that depends on the history you choose to remember.

I park in front of my place and start to clean out my car for tomorrow morning. I find a strand of hair. I hold it up to a fizzling streetlight. The strand of hair's aura alternates between gold, brown, black, gold, and I squint so hard to try and see its real color that it hurts my head. I give up and let the strand of hair fall onto the street, before a breeze snatches it from my sight. I feel myself just standing there, alone, and there's this whole city still breathing around me, sapping the air out of my lungs.

XITLALI ZARAGOZA, CURANDERA

XITLALI LEANS ON THE bar five hours into her shift at her other job as a Mexican restaurant waitress. She massages her temples and can feel the bags under her eyes deepen. A customer waves her over to his table to pay the tab for four margaritas and three cervezas, drunk and alone on a Tuesday at 5 p.m. *He has a sad aura about him, thick and gloomy, colored like cough syrup.*

"Ah-kee ten-go el dee-naro," el gringo says.

"Awesome. Thanks," Xitlali responds.

He hands over cash and barely leaves a tip. Xitlali yawns and doesn't bother to offer a blessing, as much as it seems he could use one. *Dios mío, prayers and alcohol are the two most abused inventions in human history. Any method to not completely accept this reality will do.* That's when the phone in her pocket vibrates. She walks outside and answers.

"Curandera Zaragoza, we have an assignment for you. *Es urgente.*"

"It can't wait?"

"We tried calling other curanderas, Xitlali. No one else wants to touch this."

"Why is that?" Xitlali asks, resting against the brick exterior of the Mexican restaurant and watching out for her manager.

"This client is gay. The other curanderas say they cannot save a sinner from himself. We know it's short notice, but can you take it?"

"Ay, pues . . . Of course. If evil does not discriminate, why would I?" Xitlali says as she pulls her notepad from her back pocket. *Desgraciadas.* "Dígame."

"José Benavidez has been experiencing a haunting. Says that every night, while walking home from work, there's a presence that follows him. Won't say what exactly. Says he might encounter it again tonight."

"Has there been physical interaction?"

"No."

"Bien," Xitlali mutters, scribbling onto her notepad. She can sense an energy from his name already, tense yet weakened by anxiety. *Pobrecito.* "I'll be there as soon as I can."

"Bien, bien, bien. Mira, the code is #1448 to get into the gate. Complex is called Cherry Pointe. Apartment 13."

"Gracias. Que Dios la bendiga."

"Que Dios la bendiga, Curandera Zaragoza."

After closing all her tabs and sneaking out of the restaurant an hour early, Xitlali jumps into her 2004 Ford Taurus with over 138,000 miles on the odometer and leaves for the complex fifteen minutes away. The air is thick with blaring lights like cheap, knockoff suns. Every stoplight turns red, as though trying to slow her from reaching José Benavidez. Xitlali uses these short pauses to sort through her messy back seat and work bag, both littered with clothes, various documents, and crumbs from the many dried herbs she uses day-to-day. *I gotta make time to sort through all this shit. Always something.* Juan Gabriel sings through the radio about the sadness of desire.

As Xitlali pulls up to the apartment complex's box to enter the code, she can feel music and taste food grilling. She's so hungry, she can't think of the code. Notepad out, she looks for the page, flipping through notes on other cases she's solved this last week.

*Mayra Montevideo – Heights – Curse from a Lover – Space purified
    with Sage, Oración, $40.*
*Salvador Trujillo – Midtown – Rashes from Bad Energy – Recom-
    mended oils and scents, Referred to Curandera Gabriela Herrera
    who specializes in yerberia, Oración, $20.*
*Muriel Gonzales – East End – Fevers – Blessed her belongings and
    space, Oración, $45.*

Xitlali gains some confidence, remembering she solved these
cases and many more written down in her other notepads scattered about her car's floor. *This will be no different . . . but I have a
bad feeling.*

As she parks, she sees where the sounds and smells are coming from. In the apartment complex clubhouse is a quinceañera.
Xitlali can tell from the strobe lights, cumbia pounding out from
speakers, the drunk uncle standing before a grill loaded with carne
asada, and a young woman in a light blue dress with rhinestones
lined vertically on the bustier, sequins and pearls in a swirl design
on her belly, the gown raining down the rest of her body like thin
tissue. Her silver crown peeks out of her hair, styled in a bouffant.
She's gorgeous.

A grand sadness yearns out of her heart. Xitlali hasn't spoken
to her own daughter in twelve years. She tries not to think about
it. There used to be a picture of her daughter on her dashboard,
but Xitlali took it down a while ago so as not to be reminded of
that failure. *Bad energy for the job.* She looks at the spot where
it was, a patch of plastic darker than the rest of the dashboard.
*Twelve years. Not a word. I can't do anything about it right now.
Twelve years, carajo.* Her tire bumps into the curb and wakes her
from her trance.

What makes Xitlali special is that she goes deeper than most
curanderas. Rather than just addressing the symptoms of a haunting or bad energy, she investigates what caused the problem. Her
clients love this about her.

She finds apartment 13 and knocks. She can feel a headache coming on from hunger, and her ankles are swollen from standing around all day.

"Yes?" a man yells from behind the door.

"Xitlali Zaragoza, curandera."

Locks clink behind the door before it opens.

"Come in, please," the man says. He's light-brown skinned, in his early thirties.

"José?"

"No, he's my partner. I'm Rolando. I'll let him know you're here."

There are unframed photographs all over the walls, ranging from portraits to landscapes to abstractions, some color, some black and white. One in particular stands out to Xitlali: a shoulders-up portrait of a young man. He stares at the camera—beyond it, at you—and his eyes convey a deep lethargy or an accepted sadness, if there's a difference. Xitlali stares into the picture, entranced by his eyes, which are unblinking, watching ceaselessly. *You cannot return the gaze. His gaze has power over you. That is its beauty.*

"Ms. Zaragoza, you like my self-portrait?"

Xitlali looks at the young man in the picture and the young man now standing before her. They are the same person, except that the one standing right here has an aura that isn't as strong.

"Oh, yes. I love this piece," Xitlali says.

"I took it after I had a nightmare," José says, rubbing his neck with his right hand.

Xitlali pulls out her notepad and pen. "What is this dream?"

"Can we sit down?"

"Yes, of course. But the dream. Dígame."

"Why? It's nothing really."

"If you want me to help you, you must answer my questions. Everything I ask, say, and do is to help. ¿Entiendes?"

"Yes, of course. I'm sorry."

"Don't be sorry. Go on."

"It starts with me in a room, surrounded by mirrors. I'm wearing jeans, a white shirt, and these really tall high heels. I'm staring at myself. I can't leave or move, and I work into a panic. Then my father appears and looks right at me. I can't talk. I can't do anything. Then I wake up. It's funny—in that self-portrait, I'm trying to make the face he made in the dream."

"Why do you think you have this nightmare?"

"Well, because it really happened. My dad walked in on me wearing heels as a child and gave me this angry look. They really didn't mean anything then, the heels. Just kid stuff, you know. It's the look he gave me. In the dream, it's more melancholic, but in reality, it was rage. Every time I have that dream, it reminds me of how disappointed he was in me."

"Was?"

"We stopped talking when I came out, and he died a few years ago. We never really reconciled," José says, his eyes welling up. José's partner rubs his back with one hand, but Xitlali can sense anger and helplessness form within Rolando.

Xitlali feels the same sadness from earlier creep up within her. *He must feel awful for never reconciling. It causes bad energy. I know the feeling. Shit, not right now, Xitlali.* She concentrates on the job. There's a lingering feeling of regret haunting José. *If I can find a connection, we can finish this quick.*

Rolando speaks. "This all just seems like a lot of nonsense."

"Whether you believe it or not, this is causing tangible pain and dislocation. You dismissing it only feeds the evil power. Your bad energy is wasting our time," Xitlali says. Rolando is startled and places his hand over his chest.

"I'm sorry, Ms. Zaragoza," says José. "Rolando doesn't believe any of this."

"Ya. It's okay. Look, take me to see where this happens. Then I can make an accurate assessment."

As they go to her car, Xitlali sees the party still going. She sees the birthday girl hiding behind a sedan, drinking a beer. She and the girl meet eyes for a second. Xitlali looks away. *You only get one quinceañera.*

She drives José to the movie theater where he works, a few blocks away. Its bright lights fight with the night sky long enough to attract families, couples, and loners to sit in silence together and watch. José explains that he works as a ticket attendant, sometimes as late as 1:30 a.m. He walks home alone after, in the odd time before the bars set the drunks loose but after a point of reliability for METRO buses to still be running. The homeless sleep under the bus stop kiosks. Xitlali parks in the back of the theater lot, close to the street, and directs José to lead her through his routine. She yanks her heavy work bag from the back seat, and the motion cracks off a shard of pain in her shoulder.

They walk along Westheimer, a long, long street that always smells of burnt rubber and carbon monoxide, occasionally interrupted by the aromas of foods from all over the world: Mexican, Japanese, Indian, Brazilian, Vietnamese, Chinese, Guatemalan, etc. Passing cars honk and muffled strip club music whispers through the streets. The streetlights produce a yellow glow. As Xitlali walks, she feels the looming sensation that a truck could swerve into them at any minute, or a car could pull up and drunken voices from within could call them spics, dirty Mexicans, job stealers, illegals, then step out of the car and ruin them. *A lot of dark energy here.* White bicycles and crosses dot the sidewalks, memorials where Houstonians were run over while cycling. *Conduits through which the living speak to the dead.*

"Why doesn't Rolando pick you up from work?"

"He's a bartender," José says. "So, I walk along this big street, and then I get this feeling that something is following me. I get closer to home, and this feeling of dread fills me."

"And?"

"This little stretch of road that connects Westheimer to my apartment. This is where the thing starts to follow me."

"Have you ever seen it?"

"Yes. It's hard to describe," José says, rubbing his head with his hand, trying to stimulate thought.

"Look, I know it's hard, but I have to know what it is. Otherwise, I won't be able to help you."

"Ok," José responds, massaging his left bicep with his right hand. This smaller road only goes a quarter mile, and it wallows in a murky darkness. Garbage fills the ditch alongside it. The sidewalk is cracked with no indication of future repair. There's no more sound from Westheimer.

"It's when I walk on this sidewalk that I hear them—these footsteps—clack-clack-clack." José illustrates by slapping one palm into the other.

Xitlali can sense the fear running up his spine. Blood rushes into his head, reddening his ears and cheeks. "And what do you see?" she asks.

"I'm going to sound insane."

"Mira, I've seen and heard crazy. Dígame."

"I-I look back and there's this . . . this dog. A brown-coated, white-bellied pit bull with a human face . . . this face of extreme grief. It follows me, and it's crying. What's making the clacking sound are the heels it's wearing. Bright red heels. It can walk perfectly in them, on all fours. It's sashaying, dancing even, like it's mocking my fear." A sheen of sweat gleams on José's face.

Xitlali nods. "Yes. I can feel a dark presence here. Let me inspect the area." She pulls a flashlight from her bag and uses it to illuminate sections of the sidewalk, like a prison warden searching for an escaped convict. There it is: another white cross, surrounded by fast-food wrappers, cigarette butts, and tall weeds. Xitlali approaches it and feels her pulse quicken, skin becoming cold. *Yes, this is it.* The cross has something written on it, smudged by time and rain: Gabriel Méndez. Xitlali is light-headed from the hunger and humidity and finds it harder and harder to think. *Virgen, ayúdame, porfa. Dame la fuerza.*

"Pues, José, I think I know what's happening. There was a death here—an unresolved one. Many dark feelings have lingered here and grown. It seems someone mourned this death for a moment but not enough to give this spirit peace," Xitlali explains, rubbing her temples to ward off the forming migraine. "Could be because people around here move a lot. Or they lost hope."

"What does that have to do with me?"

"You're already spiritually fatigued and carry traumas. That makes it easy for this spirit to feed off your fear and pain," Xitlali says. *I know, joven, because I, too, have a past to reconcile. Who am I to lecture anyone on that?* "You being tired after work and the fear the night instills in you make it easier for this spirit to take advantage. It's why it manifests into our reality, wearing the heels from your nightmare. It knows what gets to you. I will give this spirit peace. However, you have to make peace with whatever is happening in you, or it'll only be a matter of time before another spirit clues in on you. I can't help you with that, but I know you can do it. You must. Do you understand?"

"Yes. I understand," José says.

"Bueno. I need you to help me purify this space."

Xitlali takes the holy water from the vial on her neck and sprinkles it over the cross. She pulls some of the weeds out and collects the garbage from the ground around it. José, as instructed, places candles around the cross and lights them. Xitlali gives her minimal yet honest prayer:

> *May God bless this space,*
> *La Virgen ayúdanos,*
> *porfa, forever and always,*
> *con safos, safos, safos.*

She takes the sage from her other necklace vial and burns it to emit a fragrant smoke. She hands a piece to José, then makes the sign of the cross on herself, thumb touching left shoulder, right shoulder, forehead, and heart, then a kiss to seal it all in.

When they're done, Xitlali can sense José's energy lift from his new peace of mind. She has him sign forms and gives him her bill of sixty dollars.

Later, after she's dropped off José at his apartment complex, she sits in her car for a while to write notes.

I see more and more of these crosses along the streets. How many have been forgotten? How many spirits linger within the streets, within their cracks? As more of these traumas happen and stay unresolved, the more these restless spirits will roam within our reality and demand our attention, using our fear and anger. This spirit was more grotesque than usual and knew José's traumas, even though José did not seem to know the name on the cross. Are these spirits becoming more desperate to agitate us?

Xitlali reaches down to take off her work shoes but is interrupted by another call. She sighs before answering.

"¿Bueno?"

"Curandera Zaragoza, we have another assignment."

"I can't. I'm exhausted," Xitlali says, running her fingers through her hair.

"This is an emergency. You're the only one who can handle this case."

Puta madre. "It can't wait?"

"It's a woman and her children, and they're desperate."

Evil never rests. I can't turn down a mother and her kids. I wouldn't sleep.

"Dígame," Xitlali says.

"Trailer park out in Spring called Strawberry Glen. Contact's name is Petra Ruiz. Three daughters. Recently separated from her husband."

Fucking Spring? "Got it."

Xitlali tilts her head back and breathes in deeply. She turns on the car, opens a vial and sniffs the cinnamon and clove inside, rubs the exhaustion from her eyes, and drives. Xitlali looks at the road in front of her rather than at the spot where the picture used to be.

◎

During her drive, the purple sky becomes black. Xitlali has never been to this part of town before. Xitlali recalls hearing about these recently established communities on the outskirts of Houston from friends and colleagues, where many Latinx families settled down to provide underpaid labor and expendable energy to the growing needs of white, middle-class suburbs, Spring, The Woodlands, etc. At its outer edge, separated from the rest of the suburb by a band of tall trees, is the trailer park where her next client lives. The trailer park is so new that there are still logs stacked from all the freshly cleared trees. Proper streetlights haven't yet been installed, so generators on wheels power scattered lamps throughout the neighborhood. Cicadas scream through the hot night. Xitlali can imagine who lives here: the cooks and busboys who work in Spring's restaurants and the women who clean the mansions and schools. They live close enough to get to work but far enough from those who benefit from their work to not see them.

Xitlali drives slowly around the trailers, trying not to linger too much and cause concern. She doesn't have to wander long. Señora Ruiz sits outside the trailer with her three daughters in patio chairs, her tears falling into her bowled hands.

"Señora Ruiz? Are you Petra Ruiz?" Xitlali asks, getting out of her car.

"Sí, sí. Gracias a Dios," Petra cries, shaking Xitlali's right hand with both her own.

"Señora Ruiz, por favor, let's go back inside. It's very dark out here."

"No. No me meto con mis hijas. It's not safe in there."

The oldest daughter, around fourteen years old, has a sheathed machete in her lap, the handle resting in the grip of her fingers. She looks restless, eyes looking far into the night, and her torso rocks back and forth in her blue pajamas. Her aura is dim and purple. Her sisters play near the trailer's little light, shrouded in moths, giggling as they serve invisible tea at a small, pink table. Their auras are bright and yellow, oblivious to what's happening.

Xitlali remembers her daughter at that age. She didn't play with tea sets but collected stones and herbs, spending hours organizing them, naming them, enchanting them, getting to know each and every one. She used to beg Xitlali to bring her more during her supply runs. Then, at some point, she stopped. She turned fourteen and said she didn't want a quinceañera. She argued with Xitlali about it and gave her that look—staring at nothing, especially not at her mother. Once, she left a crystal on the windowsill to collect dust. It took a while for Xitlali to recognize how she had failed her daughter. Xitlali: came home late every night after a limpia; missed practices, award ceremonies, recitals, etc.; didn't help with homework and instead soaked herself in the bathtub.

"Why do I care about what you do, but you never care about what I like doing? Do you actually like me, or am I just your replacement?" her daughter asked finally. Xitlali doesn't remember her answer. That's when Xitlali knew her daughter didn't want this line of work. She showed it through little things: not watering her herbs, her stone collection gathering dust, rolling her eyes when Xitlali tried to teach her blessings. The last straw was Xitlali missing her high school graduation because the commission to bless a rich benefactor's mansion was too hard to pass up for Xitlali. *And then, well* . . . Xitlali forces herself to stop this train of thought, pulling out her notepad and pen. *Anyways.*

"Let's begin. The sooner we finish, the sooner everyone can go back to sleep."

"Bueno," Señora Ruiz says. "Okay, pues, let's not talk too close to mis hijas. Mijas, voy a hablar con la curandera. Aquí voy a estar. No se mueven de aquí."

"Sí, 'amá," they say in unison.

Xitlali and Petra walk to the end of the trailer. Petra leans against it and takes out a pack of cigarettes. She offers one to Xitlali before putting one between her lips and lighting it with a match. Her aura is thick and pulsating with anxiety, mostly purple and bordered with red.

"Pues, mi marido left about . . . hace two weeks, ya." Petra's eyes well up with tears. She wipes them away and takes a puff of her cigarette. "Y, pues, this started a week after he left."

"What happened?"

"On Monday, I came back into my house after seeing mis hijas off at the bus stop for school. I was getting ready for work when I felt this presence watching me," Petra says. She takes another drag of her cigarette, her exhaled smoke resembling a ghost's hand moving through the air. The smell of the smoke exacerbates Xitlali's headache. "I couldn't shake the feeling. Like someone invisible was standing in the corner, watching me. I thought I could even see it in the corners of my eyes, sabes?"

"Lo siento, pero what do you do for a living?"

"I clean houses in the neighborhood nearby."

"Okay. Go on," Xitlali says, marking it in her notes. *Typical work around here, I hear. I've been there.*

"Sí, pues, it got worse as the week went on. While we were sleeping, I'd wake up to hear breathing that didn't belong to my daughters. When I looked into the darkness, the breathing stopped, as though to hide itself. Soon, things started falling off the walls, and I started having these headaches that made me imagine the craziest things, like my daughters dying. Or from back when my own mother was sick—I think about her dying, and I can see her right in front of me, dying all over again, with her graying skin and cracking voice. I'm scared it'll get worse. Mi hija, mi mundo, my oldest tonight started crying, and I asked her, '¿Qué pasa, mi linda?' She couldn't tell me. What if she's seeing the same things? Tonight, she woke up screaming, saying she had a horrible nightmare that she doesn't want to tell me about. I brought the girls out here and called your agency. Ay, Señora Zaragoza, I can't let it get any worse. There's something muy, muy malo in this house." Petra's cigarette is now two inches of ash, ready to crumble. She struggles to get another from her pocket.

"And this all started happening after your husband left?"

"Sí, Señora. Where is he? He would know what to do. I can't afford to move out of here alone."

"If you don't mind me asking, why did your husband leave?"

"Pues, la verdad es que . . . There's a lot of reasons. He had problems with drinking, and he didn't like this place because it's so small. We started to argue a lot. What made him leave was that I told him my boss, un güero, kissed me and asked me to have sex with him. I said no, of course, but he made me promise not to tell his wife. Yo no digo nada a ella. I don't want any trouble, me entiendes?"

Ah, I see. She's disempowered at work.

"My husband told me to quit, but I said that we just moved here. The schools are good in this neighborhood, and mis hijas deserve that. It reached a point where, when he got drunk, he would keep bringing it up. He said if I wasn't going to quit or let him confront my boss, it would hurt him as a husband and man. I said no, que no, and, well, se fue."

It goes beyond the workplace. The source is her boss, but the chain continues at home. Men. No sirven para nada.

"I see. Bueno, whatever is making you see these visions could be something strong at work. I will investigate. Your husband may be involved. You don't know if he's come back? Like while you are at work?"

"I wouldn't know. Mis hijas stay with a neighbor until I get home from work at séis de la tarde."

"Does he have a key?"

"Sí, señora."

He can come and go as he pleases.

"Okay, I'm going inside."

Xitlali enters the trailer. She turns on the light and it gives a yellow tint to everything in the room. The trailer is small: a kitchen area with a sink, table, and hot plates; living room area with a love seat, shag rug, and an HD television; and the bedroom area where futons and blankets are spread across the floor, disheveled from sleep. Xitlali sees that all the pictures on the walls are warped and worn, and all the crosses look loose, ready to fall. *The good thing about this case is there isn't much to inspect.* She's tempted by the tortillas on the counter and the soft blankets on the floor. All the day's fatigue spreads through her muscles and bones like a possession. She has the urge to sit down, just for five minutes. *Get it together! Porfa, ayudame Dios.*

In the bedroom area, Xitlali feels a presence—a strong energy pushing against her. The energy travels up her arm, into her head, as though someone put a wet cloth on her brain. *Not good at all. I can see how they get visions. To someone not ready for this, it'll cause some bad shit. I have to find the source.* Xitlali looks under the futons and on the walls to see if there's any point of connection for a spirit or a conduit of evil energy. *Right there!* On a nightstand near the family's sleeping area, there is a rain lamp with oil-beaded wires surrounding a small sculpture of a tiger standing majestically at the top of a mountain; the beads of oil are suspended in place, completely still like ice. Xitlali notices a bulge near the bottom of the nightstand, where a blanket meets the floor. She lifts the blanket and sees an egg.

The egg is white and seems to be breathing. The shell strains and relaxes, emitting a sort of wheezing sound. Xitlali taps on it and a muffled sound resonates. She grabs the egg, and its shell stiffens as if it doesn't like being touched. It feels less like a shell than a layer of warm skin. *What the hell is this thing?* Xitlali picks at the shell. The white peels off, and the egg begins bleeding. The egg's energy surges through her body. *Fuck!* She feels it release more energy. She can't fight it. An exhaustion seizes her body . . .

I see someone off in the white distance. It's my daughter! I see her as she is now. She's so gorgeous. Her brown hair is long, reaching down to her lower back. She's aging like me, Dios mío. I don't miss seeing her father's nose. She's wearing nice jeans and a green sweater. Ay, she's always wearing the wrong thing! It's summer! Ay mija why do you always wear a sweater in the summer? Pues, I guess it doesn't matter. She's here! Mi vida, she's here! She seems to be talking to people.

I'm going to walk up to her and surprise her. Mija! It's me! Tu mamá, la única que tienes. Dígame! Tell me everything. Oh, how I've missed you. Dígame todo. ¿Qué pasa? What are you doing now? Where do you work? Where do you live? Are you seeing anyone? You're not married, are you? And your studies? Hey, por qué . . . why are you looking at me like that? That's no way to look at your only mother. Twelve years and this is how we start? No me mires así. Mija, where are you going? Where have you been all these years? Please, mija. Don't go. If I reach out to you, will you hold me? I'm trying to hug you, mija, but you only go further away. Please stop looking at me like that. Please stop going away. I can't take it. No seas cruel, mija. I can't see your face. I can't. I can't . . .

Someone bangs at the trailer door. Xitlali opens her eyes and finds herself lying on the floor, on the blankets.

"Señora Zaragoza! Is everything okay?"

"Yes!"

How long was I out? Holy shit, that was strong.

Xitlali sits up and rubs the tears from her face. She sees the egg lying where she dropped it, on the blanket next to her. *Whoever did this really wanted this family gone.*

Xitlali takes a pair of tweezers from her bag and uses them to remove a tiny figurine from the vial on her necklace. She places the figurine on top the egg, says a bendición, and gives it time to absorb the egg's spell. Then she burns sage near the egg. The smoke surrounds the egg but doesn't touch it, pushed away by dense energy. Xitlali waits a bit, then uses the tweezers to pick up the figurine and hold it near the burning sage. Like the egg, the figurine repels the smoke. *The energy transfer was a success.* The beads of oil on the lamp's wires are moving again, infinitely dripping top to bottom and bending light so the room's surfaces warp. Tears of melted glass envelop the tiger.

She puts the figurine back into the vial. She puts the egg in a black pouch with sage, rosemary, and hierba santa. She blesses both egg and figurine. As Xitlali steps out of the trailer, she thinks about advising Señora Ruiz to leave. But she knows that if the woman could do so, she would've already. There's no use telling her the obvious. *There's only so much we can come to terms with. Así es . . .*

Instead, she says, "Someone cursed an egg and placed it near your beds, Señora Ruiz. It was a strong curse, done by someone either inexperienced or evil. Your daughter must have slept too close to it tonight, causing her nightmares. I got rid of it, but someone put it there. I don't want to say it's your husband, but that's the only person I can think of. He may have paid someone to place the curse. I don't know. What I'm saying is, it's gone for now, but he might do it again. You need to talk to him and tell him he's hurting your daughters."

"Thank you, Señora Zaragoza. Gracias, gracias, gracias," Petra cries.

"Claro, señora. Bueno, let's all get in a circle." The family gathers and Xitlali has them clasp hands. *Do they know any of this? Is it better for the little ones to not know? Perhaps if you don't believe in these things, they have less power over you. Maybe it's best if my kind die out. Ay, mija . . . Maybe you were right.*

Xitlali recites the prayer:

May God bless this house,
La Virgen ayúdanos,
porfa, forever and always,
con safos, safos, safos.

She tells Señora Ruiz how to purify the trailer with sage, hierba santa, and rosemary, every day, for as long as they have to live there. Señora Ruiz signs the standard form for purification services and pays the $40 bill in cash.

"Gracias, gracias, Curandera. If it weren't so late, I'd invite you in for café."

"'Stá bien. Take care of your hijas. Their fear only provides more dark energy for evil spirits. Love them. Dales todo."

"Claro que sí."

In her car, Xitlali watches the Ruiz family walk back into the trailer, one by one. She wonders if they will be safe.

Her gente, spreading into spaces where they weren't allowed before, opening new traumas and wounds that will take years and lifetimes and generations to even diagnose. New manifestations of spirits, dark energy, and evil permeate our reality, evolving within these transitions. Then comes the work of accepting past truths. Reconciliation. She will always have work. There will always be a need for her services.

I'm so tired.

Xitlali drives back into the city on the great spine of the freeway that connects the suburbs, where people like her work and clean, to the skyscrapers, where people like her work and clean. The drive feels like a dream, the passing billboards and landscapes acting as newsreels for the imagination. Over yonder, the light from the sleepless metropolis fights with the darkness of the cosmos above.

Xitlali will drive these freeways many times over the coming years. She will take her daughter's picture from the glove box and tape it, again, to her dashboard. It would behoove her to come to peace with herself, her past, with what she's done. That's another story. For now, Xitlali Zaragoza, curandera, will rest as much as she can until her next assignment.

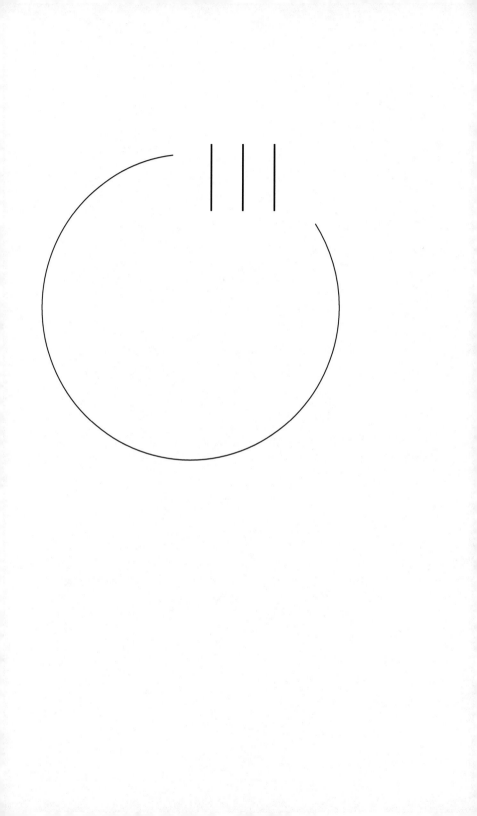

XIMENA DELUNA
V.
THE NEW MARS TERRITORY

IN THE DISTRICT COURT OF
THE NEW MARS TERRITORY

XIMENA DELUNA,
    Plaintiff,
    v.
GOVERNMENT OF THE NEW MARS TERRITORY
Defendant.

COMPLAINT

1. This action is authorized by Title 42, United States Code, section 1981, providing for the equal rights of citizens and of all other persons within the jurisdiction of the United States.

    2. This is a proceeding for a declaratory judgment and injunction to determine:

(a) Whether the United States New Mars Territory's (USNMT) actions are unconstitutional in that it organizes and maintains facilities and services for the education and welfare of white children and denies said facilities and services for the nonwhite child of a Mantenedor in the Solis Planum of the USNMT.

(b) The question of whether the plaintiff's child has been denied, solely because of race, resources afforded to white children at educational facilities situated in the Solis Planum of the USNMT and thus violates the Fourteenth Amendment to the Constitution of the United States.

3. (a) DeLuna's child is a citizen of the United States, born in the Jackson Memorial Hospital of the Solis Planum of the USNMT. DeLuna's child is the first human being officially born in the New Mars Territory since its establishment eight years ago. In fact, no person, on record, has been able to give birth on Mars. Experts and researchers theorize that the radiation present on Mars, despite the infrastructure that makes life possible and sustainable within the territory's confines, permeates down to the molecular level; pregnancies usually do not go to full term. Hence, all children present on the territory were brought in from Earth after two years of initial colonization stages. That is, until DeLuna gave birth to her child five years ago.

Up until the child's fifth birthday, DeLuna was able to raise her child through agreements with other Mantenedores to keep the child hidden when she reported for work duty. According to witnesses and firsthand testimonies, many members of the Mantenedor community took it upon themselves to care for the child as the birth was seen as a miracle. USNMT government officials were unaware of all this until the plaintiff decided to enroll the child into school on their fifth birthday. It was then that the USNMT denied DeLuna's child access to basic education, a right guaranteed by the Fourteenth Amendment.

The reasons for denying the child access to basic education given by various representatives of the USNMT at different times were egregious and shall be enumerated upon later. Thus far, the child has been afforded a subpar "distance" education, and an additional fee was subtracted from the plaintiff's pay to compensate for "the cost of special education," a violation of the Equal Protection Clause. The plaintiff reports that her child is provided with educational videos that are outdated and racist. For example, one of the educational videos provided argues that "civil rights groups adopted a revolutionary narrative that sought the destruction of Western civilization," "mass migration from Latin America has caused crime and exploitation detrimental to the United States," and it refers to slaves simply as "workers." The white children do not watch this video as part of their curriculum. As a result, the plaintiff's child does not and cannot receive educational advantages, opportunities, and facilities equal to those given to white children.

(b) Ximena DeLuna, from El Salvador, is not a U.S. citizen but is a resident of, domiciled in, and pays all taxes of the USNMT and the U.S. as a contracted worker. DeLuna arrived on the USNMT six years ago as part of the second wave of contracted laborers hired to build, service, and maintain infrastructure necessary for the colony's survival. Nearly 93% of all contracted workers on the USNMT are non–U.S. citizens as a result of the latest trade agreement between the U.S. and several Central American countries (such as El Salvador, Honduras, Guatemala, Nicaragua, and Belize) that provides laborers with shelter, salary, healthcare, and food at a minimal cost. This agreement is more commonly known as the Mantenedor Program. However, applicants with children were disqualified from the program. Hence, DeLuna's miraculous pregnancy and birth of her child is important in establishing a precedent of USNMT citizenship.

DeLuna was a factory worker in El Salvador but currently works as a grid operator at the USNMT Energy Center, which is responsible for the day-to-day output of energy to all USNMT infrastructure. Like all the other contract laborers, DeLuna lives in the Blue Wing of the USNMT in a designated residence area, separate from

U.S. citizens and researchers/scientists to maximize workflow efficiency. As in, all contracted laborers are assigned barrack-like living quarters close to all labor-centric facilities that do not intersect with research or science facilities. All training occurs on-site, and the living quarters are entirely self-sufficient with medical facilities, refectories, and food dispensaries. It was in this context that DeLuna became pregnant.

(c) As stated, carrying a pregnancy to term was seen as impossible amongst USNMT inhabitants, and the laborers took communal care of the child out of reverence. Once the child reached the age of five, DeLuna was encouraged by her community to enroll the child in school as the resources in the designated living quarters are not equipped with education materials for children. The USNMT's Green Wing maintains a full library, classrooms, and state-of-the-art learning tools. In essence, the Mantenedores understood the child would be at a disadvantage later in life if not given full access to all the educational opportunities the USNMT holds. Thus, the plaintiff brings this action on her child's behalf and on behalf of all persons similarly situated within the USNMT, now and forever forward.

4. The USNMT has declared education as a state function integral to its foundation, pursuant to the New Mars Territory Constitution, Education Code, Title 2, Subtitle A, Chapter 4, Section 4.001, which states, "The New Mars Territory, founded as a research and science colony in pursuit of knowledge that advances American interests, declares that any educational institution undertaking to provide education, services, or activities to any individual within the jurisdiction or geographical boundaries of the educational institution shall provide equal opportunities to all *citizens* within its jurisdiction or geographical boundaries free of charge, pursuant to this code." However, the USNMT does not provide the Blue Wing with any schools since Title 1, Chapter 1, Section 1.003 states, "An educational institution may not deny services to any individual eligible to participate in a school district's education program . . ." The keyword is "eligible" as noncitizens, chiefly the Mantenedores,

are considered "ineligible." Therefore, there hasn't been a "need" to establish K-12 schools since Title 2, Subtitle A, Chapter 4, Section 4.002 states, "The general diffusion of knowledge is essential for the welfare of this state and for the preservation of the liberties and rights of *citizens*." The USNMT provides impeccable educational tools and opportunities to citizens and their children, all brought in from the mainland and thus pre-approved. But the USNMT did not anticipate a citizen to be born from a noncitizen on the USNMT.

5. All schools within the USNMT are under the control and supervision of the defendants.

(a) The USNMT was primarily founded to facilitate science and research on further terraforming the surface of Mars for larger-scale populations. As stated, institutions of education are inherently part of the functions of the USNMT to ensure progress and real-time development of future scholars. Research facilities on the USNMT are frequently staffed by, are in partnership with, or are on loan from educational bodies such as universities, hospitals, and/or research centers on Earth, with the intent to establish local, permanent institutions of education.

(b) The Government of the New Mars Territory is under a duty to: enforce the laws of the USNMT, maintain an efficient system of public schools in the USNMT, determine the studies pursued and the methods of teaching, and establish such schools as may be necessary to the completeness and efficiency of the school system. The educational system of the USNMT is inseparable from the Government and therefore declared by law to be a body corporate and is sued in its governmental capacity.

(c) All educational institutions on the USNMT, seeing as they are inseparable from government, are funded by taxes and tariffs imposed on all people present on the USNMT, citizens and Mantenedors alike. Hence, all educational institutions on the USNMT are free of charge to all citizens as long as they are "eligible." No Mantenedor, on the basis of citizenship, is "eligible" for free education. That may change.

6. 100% of all 2,062 U.S. citizens on the USNMT are white, according to the latest census two years ago, which does not include DeLuna's child. 100% of all 2,526 participants in the Mantenedor program are nonwhite. All 362 citizens under the age of eighteen on the USNMT are white. Therefore, all licensed teachers and eligible students on the USNMT are white, save for DeLuna's child. All citizens present on the USNMT were approved by a committee, serving on behalf of the Federal government, whose members are all white. The denial of DeLuna's child to an equal education is a structural and deliberate effort.

7. DeLuna's attempts to enroll her child in an educational program have been met with conflict, denial, and unequal accommodation, all in violation of the child's rights under the Fourteenth Amendment of the Constitution of the United States.

(a). The first recorded attempt by DeLuna to enroll her child into school had her having to prove the child was born on the USNMT. Since DeLuna did not birth her child in a hospital of the USNMT, no official birth certificate had been issued. DeLuna did not birth her child in a hospital since she was denied access to a healthcare professional during her delivery. According to an official report taken by a USNMT medical professional on duty at the time, several Mantenedores attempted to have a medical professional tend to DeLuna's delivery. However, the medical professional on duty took this as a joke since, again, it was "impossible" for a child to be born on Mars. Still, a report was filed. Fortunately, the delivery was corroborated by photographic and video evidence on-site by several Mantenedores tending to DeLuna's delivery. It was only when a committee conducted an official investigation into the evidence brought forth by twelve Mantenedores, all evidence with time-stamps that match up with the recorded timestamp of the official report, that a birth certificate was issued.

(b) The second attempt to enroll DeLuna's child in the education system was met with denial due her child being marked as "ineligible" on the grounds of lacking the intellectual aptitude to meet the educational standards of the USNMT Kindergarten program. DeLuna's child is proficient in speaking, reading, and writing English, Spanish, and one unidentified Indigenous language. This rationale alone is disproved on the grounds that DeLuna's child knows more languages than 83% of all U.S. citizens on the USNMT and 100% of all citizens under the age of eighteen on the USNMT. The child's language competency is corroborated by testing issued by the USNMT.

(c) The third and final attempt to enroll DeLuna's child into the educational program has resulted in the current situation. After DeLuna proved the child's citizenship and aptitude, the Government of the New Mars Territory claimed that the child's "health status" deemed them ineligible since they were a "medical anomaly"; they claim that the child might be mutated due to radiation and, therefore, a possible carrier of untraceable and/or dormant diseases. The only way to clear DeLuna's child from these claims was for her to surrender custody of the child to the Government of the New Mars Territory for testing and observation for an indefinite period of time. Upon her refusal, DeLuna's child was barred from enrolling in USNMT schools.

The compromise reached was that, for the "safety" of the white children and educators in the Green Wing, DeLuna's child would be taught separately in the Blue Wing through a distance education program. However, this education program does not allow for DeLuna's child to have access to the Green Wing's educational resources, opportunities, and facilities that are provided to all the white children residing within the USNMT. All this is despite DeLuna paying for this accommodation through a "special education fee" that is garnished from her wages every month. When asked if they ever planned to build educational facilities in the Blue Wing, the USNMT stated: "It is not within the USNMT's purview to establish such facilities for noncitizens." This is in violation of DeLuna's child's rights under the Fourteenth Amendment of the Constitution of the United States.

8. Therefore, DeLuna's child is being willfully and unlawfully discriminated against by the defendant on account of their race, in that the plaintiff's child is being denied the right to an equal education as the white children experience; DeLuna's child is being deprived of rights guaranteed by the Constitution and laws of the United States.

9. The plaintiff's child is suffering irreparable injury by reason of the acts herein complained of that will cause further, irreparable injury not only to the plaintiff's child but to all those in the future in similar circumstances.

WHEREFORE, the plaintiff demands that:

1. The Court enter a judgment declaring that the actions taken by the USNMT are unconstitutional insofar as they empower defendants to set up an unequal education program that violates DeLuna's child's rights, and presumably those of all possible future generations, under the equal protection clause of the U.S. Constitution.

2. The Court issue a permanent injunction forever restraining the defendants from denying all nonwhite children equal opportunities, facilities, and resources provided by the USNMT's free education system.

3. The Court retain jurisdiction of this cause after judgment to render such relief in the future, a precedent set forth by the landmark cases such as *Mendez, et al. v. Westminster* (1947) and *Brown v. Board of Education* (1954), because it has not been in the nature of the justice and educational systems to correct themselves without those vigilantly fighting for equality.

By

Ricardo Falfurrias

Attorney for Plaintiff

THE LATINX PARADOX WITHIN
JOAQUÍN SALVATIERRA

Latin[x]s live longer than Caucasians . . . Scientists refer to this as the "[Latinx] paradox" . . . Our study helps explain this by demonstrating that Latin[x]s age more slowly at the molecular level.

—STEVE HORVATH, DAVID GEFFEN SCHOOL
OF MEDICINE AT UNIVERSITY OF CALIFORNIA
LOS ANGELES, QUOTED IN UCLA NEWSROOM

JOAQUÍN SALVATIERRA LOOKS UP at the sky that resembles an alligator's eye. He doesn't like staring into the iris too long as it feels like a god is watching everything decay and can't care to do anything. "Ya, se acabó todo, joven," Joaquín's first sergeant, Fernando Monserrat, once lamented before whistling and kicking the dirt beneath his foot. "Los muertos van a caminar sobre la tierra porque ya está lleno el infierno."

In Joaquín's defense, whatever is left in front of him isn't much more hopeful to look at either. The thing about his Mk. 12 suit is that even though it's a slower and heavier model than the Mk. 11, the .50 caliber minigun upgrade built into its arm shreds a body like a tomato in a blender. In fact, Joaquín has the only Mk. 12 suit in his squad and is testing its first-ever use in the field. Joaquín's squad mates nicknamed the mecha suit "El Joderoso." And, true to its name, what remains of Lt. Charles Armstrong is absolutely fucked up beyond all recognition. The plates of Lt. Armstrong's Mk. 6 could barely repel the bullets from a standard 7.62x51 heavy machine gun, so the .50 caliber left behind enough scraps of meat, metal, and blood to put half a man back together again, all pooled up in the crater created by the bullets. Everyone in Joaquín's squad is speechless until Pvt. Julio Guevara breaks the silence.

"What the fuck was that? ¡No jodas, man! ¡Hiciste un pinche desmadre, Salvatierra!" Pvt. Guevara yells. Joaquín stifles a laugh, hearing Julio freaking out over the radio but Julio's mecha standing absolutely still. Joaquín doesn't respond and can only think about the consequences of his actions. He looks up at the eye again, tries to think of how he'll explain this to his superiors. Though the incident could be chalked up to a malfunction in Joaquín's mecha suit, it is protocol that the transgression of one Hispanic overrules all their other qualities of the squad. Joaquín must get his story straight. This is what he has so far:

You see, what happened was that as our squad (comprised of myself, Sgt. Monserrat, Pvt. Guevara, Specialist Gómez, and Lt. Armstrong) was running reconnaissance, sirs, an enemy insurgent fired a rocket that hit Spc. Gómez directly. We returned fire and neutralized all targets. Spc. Gómez reported feeling unwell. Lt. Armstrong implored continuing recon. An hour or so later, sirs, Spc. Gómez stated that he could no longer continue. Lt. Armstrong ran his vitals and found no irregularities in the report Spc. Gómez's Mk. 9 produced. Lt. Armstrong ordered Spc. Gómez to press on. I don't recall how much time elapsed until Spc. Gómez's suit powered down. He then communicated that the force of the rocket must have ruptured one of his organs because a great pain in his gut prevented him from being able to control the suit. We then noticed that blood seeped out of a crack in his armor. Lt. Armstrong ran another report on his Mk. 9 and agreed that that was what must've happened.

During the report, Spc. Gómez died. Lt. Armstrong noted this and demanded the return of the suit for repair. When Sgt. Monser-

*rat inquired on what to do about Spc. Gómez's body, Lt. Armstrong
ordered it removed from the suit. Lt. Armstrong overrode the controls
of Spc. Gómez's Mk. 9 and opened its entry hatch. Blood poured out
in steaming heaps, trailing out of his eyes, ears, nose, and mouth. Spc.
Gómez's eyes remained open. Lt. Armstrong then ordered Pvt. Guevara
to remove Spc. Gómez's body. Pvt. Guevara hesitated. When Pvt. Guevara did not fulfill his directive, Lt. Armstrong threatened to have him
killed. Lt. Armstrong then ordered Sgt. Monserrat to raise his weapon
at Pvt. Guevara and fire when he counted down from three. If he didn't,
then Lt. Armstrong would have Sgt. Monserrat court-martialed. Three.
Sgt. Monserrat did not raise his weapon. Two. Pvt. Guevara still did
not move. One. Lt. Armstrong raised his weapon at Sgt. Monserrat. I
can't recall what happened next. I remember hearing a swarm of bees.
I regained control afterward.*

"So, you're saying it's the suit's fault?" Joaquín can imagine one
of his superiors asking with a raised eyebrow. "Yes," he sees himself
saying like a fucking idiot. "Could not be helped. Not my fault." *Yes.
Great. Fantastic.*

"Está bien, mijo. Todo bien," Sgt. Monserrat finally assures,
chanting over and over on the squad's frequency, "Todo bien. Tran-
quilo, mijo. Todo bien." Spc. Gómez is still in his suit, his body all
out of blood. A red light blinks near his contorted face, indicating
the suit is still operational but out of energy. He seems to be deeply
sleeping now, so deep that it hurts. The gore and bits of Lt. Armstrong droop off rocks and leaves. "Está bien. Todo bien, mijo."

"What the fuck are we going to do, Sgt. Monserrat, sir?" Pvt.
Guevara still asks. It's a good question as there are many timelines
that can sprout from here.

> 1. Sgt. Fernando Monserrat would face a court-martial for
> being the highest-ranking Hispanic member of the squad and
> having a white man die under his direction. Though Lt. Arm-
> strong was in command, the responsibility lies entirely with

Sgt. Monserrat to keep other Hispanics under control. The suits
have on record that Sgt. Monserrat hesitated in carrying out his
order, making it clear that not keeping Pvt. Guevara in check
is what led to Joaquín's malfunction. Sgt. Monserrat would be
stripped of his rank, pay, pension, and be assigned work until
death. His family, a wife and three children, would be left
destitute.

2. Joaquín Salvatierra would simply be killed. His killing of a
white man would not be tolerated by white soldiers. Perhaps
Salvatierra could make the argument that the suit had drained
him of his energy and faculties, but his near-instinctual killing
of a white man would run contrary to all his training and
programming. To absolve Joaquín's killing of Lt. Armstrong
for his larger usefulness would be to admit that a brown man's
contributions meant more than a white life.

3. Pvt. Guevara would be court-martialed and sentenced to
labor until death. *And those are the best-case scenarios.* The cre-
ativity of cruelty by the whites is not something Joaquín wants
to imagine.

Once, his superiors ordered all the Hispanic troops to file up in
formation and watch an AWOL soldier march naked outside. The
air slowly stripped away his skin by pieces. He collapsed, and his
body decayed at five times the speed a normal body decomposes.
His particles rose to the sky, like rain from the ground sucked into
clouds.

Sgt. Monserrat is the first to move. He walks over to Spc.
Gómez's body and raises his suit's right arm above Spc. Gómez's
Mk. 9, pointer fingertip touching thumb. He then brings his arm
down, maintaining the connection of his two robotic digits, swings
it upward to the left, then cuts it straight across to the right. Sgt.
Monserrat returns his arm to the center of this cross he conjured
and releases his digits. He says, "Que Dios bendiga Arturo Gómez."
Bendiga? What is that? Joaquín has never seen or heard anything like

this. All the other Hispanic soldiers he's seen die were disposed of like buckets of bullet casings. *Is this what it's supposed to be like?* Pvt. Guevara asks again, "What are we going to do?"

"Qué quieres que te diga," Sgt. Monserrat answers.

"Anything, hombre. Shit, lie to me. Tell me we're going to be okay. ¡Algo!"

"Te calmas o te calmo, Guevara. Salvatierra, dígame."

"Diga—what? I . . . I don't understand," Joaquín says. He had never heard that word either.

"Ponte las pilas, Salvatierra. No hay mucho tiempo."

More phrases Joaquín didn't understand. All Joaquín could think about is what life he lived that led to this moment. He doesn't feel bad for shooting Lt. Armstrong. A breeze blows across his body even though his suit is sealed shut. The alligator's eye stares down at all this.

◎

Joaquín Salvatierra can't remember when or where he was born. His earliest memory is sitting in a classroom with other students in a pure white room wearing white jumpsuits. Their brown skin stood out. Their nametags hung on black string lanyards. On a whiteboard, a white teacher taught them in black marker: math, science, history, English. $2 + 2 = 4$; a sentence contains a subject and a verb; the New United States formed in 2050. Joaquín and his classmates noticed the names mentioned in their historical education were nothing like theirs. Looking back, Joaquín realized that the first mistake in all this was letting everyone keep their names: Soledad Villalobos, Xiomara DeLuna, Noe Martínez, Alejandro Cienfuegos, etc. The second was allowing them to speak Spanish to facilitate communication between nonwhite soldiers and white officers if need be. When not in the classroom, Joaquín and his classmates were in their white rooms or training. They were taught everything about the suits. *You enter them by stepping up the knee plate, turning around, and falling backwards into its ten-foot frame. You must make sure the suit's seal is secure as the ozone has eroded. Wait until the interface boots up and links to with your brain's patterns. This results in a half second of lag between a user's will and the suit's action. Through this brain link, each suit in a squad is connected to a neural network to operate cohesively as a unit.*

Joaquín's first suit was the Mk. 6, the very model Lt. Armstrong wore, which included a square head-up display inside the helmet. At this time, white soldiers could only operate the Mk. 3. Any models above required extensive training for years, which severely limited the speed and scope of the *Reconquista*, the New United States' campaign to colonize Mars. It was discovered that Hispanic soldiers piloted the suits for much longer and more accurately. No explanation could be found for this phenomenon. When Joaquín and his classmates operated the Mk. 6 at the age of fourteen, the research and development of mecha suits expanded exponentially.

The Mk. 11 that Sgt. Monserrat wields as an adult was released only a year prior to this moment; Joaquín had tested and mastered it by age seventeen. The main difference between models is how much energy each suit requires from its user. The higher the suit model, the more efficiently the suit's battery could hold a charge from a human body. The Mk. 12 carries out Joaquín's thoughts into motions instantaneously, operating more as an extension of himself.

In a way, Joaquín knew what was going to happen today. He'd worked with Sgt. Monserrat before. Sgt. Monserrat was fighting to become a full person, a deal extended by the New United States to nonwhites if they served in the *Reconquista* for twenty years. Sgt. Monserrat told Joaquín he knew that the deal was basura, that no one like him survives that long. "Cada persona tiene su número aquí," he said.

"Why are you doing this, then?" Joaquín asked.

"Esta tierra ya no es para los humanxs, joven. Los demonios corren todx, y yo hago lo que tengo que hacer para sobrevivir."

Joaquín's relation to Sgt. Monserrat was always tenuous because he sensed that Sgt. Monserrat never said everything. *I don't think he even believes all that.* Though Joaquín didn't fully trust Sgt. Monserrat, he still felt attached to el viejo because only he knew the closest thing to a reality before the current world they lived in.

"El cielo era azul, y tuvimos un dios." *Did we?*

Before embarking on today's mission, Sgt. Monserrat gave Joaquín a necklace with a pendant that resembled a plus sign.

"Ya no me sirve más, joven. No good. Tómelo, hasta que ya no lo necesites."

Then what good is it to me? However, Joaquín appreciated this totem that made them both bigger than before. He'd never felt something like this and wanted to protect it. When Lt. Armstrong raised his weapon against Sgt. Monserrat, Joaquín witnessed each bullet puncture Armstrong's suit and tear flesh from bone like a flower's petals into the wind before it came to pass only nanoseconds later.

Maybe there are no mistakes.

◎

"Ya. Te tienes que ir, mijo," Sgt. Monserrat says to wake Joaquín from his trance. "Vete."

"They'll kill you straight up," Pvt. Guevara chimes in. "Take the suit and run."

"What about you two?" Joaquín asks.

"Yo tengo familia que no puedo abandonar. Un día me uniré contigo, pero hoy no. Te lo juro. Vete, mijo. Ya no hay más que este país te puede dar," Sgt. Monserrat says.

Joaquín Salvatierra finally feels conflicted about something. He knows he is nothing more than a means to an end for his country, but he is scared to leave it. But Sgt. Monserrat is right.

"You said there were others like you, right?" Pvt. Guevara asks Joaquín. "Maybe link up with them. We'll say enemies captured you and killed Armstrong. They can't recover his footage now that you've turned him into liquid shit. Sgt. Monserrat can do a wipe of our footage since he's in command. It's a one-in-a-million situation, man. Take advantage of it."

"Empieza algo nuevo, mijo."

After they leave, Joaquín Salvatierra ponders what to do next. He doesn't think trying to connect with his classmates is a bad idea. Theoretically, he could patch into the other Mk. 12's unique frequencies, but that would take time. For now, Joaquín has to get his thoughts straight. *I am of a nation, but I cannot be it. Of what use is that to me?*

"Joaquín? Is that you?" Joaquín's HUD brightens, and a panel opens to show a live video feed from inside Xiomara DeLuna's suit. It's her face. Xiomara is special. Everyone knows that from the moment they lay eyes on her. Her most distinguishing feature is a mole between her eyes. In class the instructors would force her to cover it up as rumors spread that it gives her power. *If anyone could've figured out how to connect suit frequencies this fast, it would be Xiomara.*

"Xiomara? Yeah, it's me."

"We have to talk. Whatever you do, don't go back to base."

"I'm way ahead of you on that," Joaquín says.

"Good. Here are my coordinates. Going to try to patch in others. Meet me ASAP."

"Will do. Be careful." The feed ends.

This could all be a trap. Who knows who is on which side? Maybe the others will force us to go back. What if I have to raise my weapon at one of us? He heads to Xiomara's coordinates. *What else do I have?* He remembers the pendant Sgt. Monserrat gave him, the two intersecting lines. *There are no mistakes.*

Joaquín looks up at the alligator's eye. It is still up there, staring down at him. He breathes in with anxiety and exhales with hope, like a pitcher overflowing with water. The eye closes.

AN ADVENTURE OF XUXA, LA ÚLTIMA

XUXA, LA ÚLTIMA, LOOKS through her binoculars from a hill and sees a large, makeshift wall made of rotting wood, tin fencing, car doors, and other scrap material. A single guard patrols it with an old rifle, clearly tired based on the slouch in her posture. Xuxa looks past her and notices some midsize buildings, people coming in and out of them. *Small settlement, six to eight families, some crops, no livestock. Not visible, anyway. Minimal fortifications. Could be overrun within minutes, easy, like this place never existed.*

Upon finding any settlement of survivors in this wasteland, Xuxa, La Última, asks herself a grave question: *Do I let them know or do I let them burn?* It's a big question, absolutely, so Xuxa has this process, imperfect but available, where she arrives at an answer.

First, La Última approaches their gates and asks to be accepted. If she's rejected, she lets Mil Fuegos's army of the undead, consisting of thousands of zombies, descend upon them. After all, how can she save any community if they won't even let her in? This happens often. La Última moves on to the next settlement and looks back to see the thick flames of a burning community dancing through the night sky.

If she's allowed in, La Última follows their orders. On her person, they will find: a handsome, pump-action shotgun (nicknamed La Escupeta for how the sixteen-inch barrel spits out shot); fourteen shells (which look like enlarged seeds); binoculars; a clean machete; cans of food (some expired, some for dogs or cats); an extendable baton; a small vial of burnt sage on a string that she wears around her neck; a full bottle of tequila (perhaps the last one since the agave died); a sewing kit; some torn books; and patches of leather and fabric (to repair the soles of her boots or holes in her clothes). They ask her questions. She responds with half-truths.

"Porfa, my name is [insert fake name here], and I'm tired of wandering," she answers.

What she will not tell them unless they pass her test is that in a few days, Mil Fuegos and his army of zombies will arrive, knock down their walls, eat their people, raze their settlement, erase their history, and absorb their lives to increase the ranks of the undead army so that Mil Fuegos may continue his genocide upon the human race.

Upon being welcomed, Xuxa attempts to assimilate into their society. She takes notes. She evaluates these communities based on one question: Is this society looking to rebuild the Earth with hope and love, creating a "new and sweeping utopia of life, where no one will be able to decide for others how they die, where love will prove true and happiness be possible"?

Usually when Xuxa is taken to meet a community's leader, a quick process follows where guards escort her to a stern yet concerned man who lays the ground rules for assimilation, tired yet tested clichés such as, "If you don't work, you don't eat"; "Everyone contributes what they can"; "There are no free meals"; "This is not a democracy"; etc., etc. If the society has *potential* to create a fair and just society, *though nothing is perfect*, Xuxa concedes, she will reveal more half-truths: "A man by the name of Mil Fuegos comes and you cannot stop him. He will kill you all. Do what you will with this information." Xuxa has never seen a community pack up and leave, which is the right answer. *You simply cannot defeat Mil Fuego's undead army; it numbers in the thousands, does not need rest, has no rules of occupation or engagement, and has no intention of leaving anything alive.* Xuxa can say all this, but can a society so selfish and self-centered as not to run away truly thrive? *This is what must have doomed us in the first place,* Xuxa believes. *Our inability to move on to save ourselves.*

Right before Xuxa escapes, prior to the arrival of Mil Fuegos's army, she witnesses communities anchor down (that is, if they believed her) and rev up the presence of armaments and patrols, all hands on deck to defend, etc., to stop the onslaught. It's never worked. La Última looks back in the night, miles away, and there the flames are. Xuxa always came to be La Última.

Xuxa wasn't always this pessimistic. There was a point when she believed every community, ideology, and people had a right to exist, even in the face of the postapocalypse. "We're better than all this," she'd say, looking at the moon and the stars, thinking past the ruins, the bones, the rotting meat, the dying people, the living dead. But then something happened.

◎

Xuxa woke up, shotgun ready, in a car the color of an old turtle shell, stirred from sleep by a zombie trying to eat their way through the back passenger door, yawning and yawning over and over, black blood and old skin smeared across the window, tearing away pieces of a face, exposing bone and molars. Xuxa imagined the life this one had before becoming this thing: perhaps a parent, perhaps a hunter, perhaps a member of a community destroyed long ago and now exiled into this horror of unliving. *What a fucking life.* When she sat up, however, she saw that the zombie's torso was slathered in red paint, front and back. That's when she knew: Mil Fuegos's army was four, maybe five, days away. He employed a system of sending out scout zombies like echolocation, measuring the time from when he sent out a scout to an area he suspected of holding a settlement to when he found it. If he caught up to the scout, the less likely there was a settlement; if he didn't catch up to it, then he surmised that it must've been captured or killed, perhaps indicating human activity and worth culling his army to converge upon a location. *One or two times not being able to find a scout is a coincidence, three times calls for an investigation*, he'd say.

Xuxa put on her boots, shook her head violently to wake herself up, ate an apple she had found from a tree nearby the night before, and checked her map for possible areas nearby most likely to be fertile for settlements. The map was old, older than her. *It's not likely entire landscapes could've changed since all this started. He must be headed here*, she thought, looking at what appeared to be a suburban neighborhood. She had seen a string of smoldering homes about a week ago, filled with charred corpses, half devoured, the rest perhaps joined Mil Fuegos's ranks. *Looking to clear these suburbs out, just as I suspected. About a few miles ahead.* Xuxa stared out the windshield at the road ahead with thick, brown grass on both sides, so long and dry in some areas that it wilted under its own weight, primed for a fire. Xuxa had developed the skill to identify what can still get worse in the world.

Xuxa opened the car door opposite the one the zombie gnawed at and kicked the window, one, two, three times to break it, allowing the zombie to crawl in. Xuxa was already out the other door, and she walked around to where the zombie had woken her and waited. It turned around to exit back out the broken window, headfirst, to which Xuxa responded by slicing through its neck with her machete. Its head bounced pitifully and rested on the asphalt like a half-deflated ball. Then, another zombie stumbled up to the car from the grass. Then another, and another. Several zombies rose from the tall, brown grass, like rotten flowers unwilting. *Me breaking the glass must've alerted them. I should've fucking scouted better, but I was so tired.*

¡No mames! Xuxa, the person she is, knowing what she knows now, wouldn't have been this sloppy. Xuxa ran down the single road. Xuxa ran and ran. *It could take a few hours to get there. I have to warn them that he's coming.* Knowing what she knows now . . .

It's too late. More emerged alongside the road in a perfect line, seemingly planted there. They snapped at her, snarling and crying, as though they needed to feast on Xuxa to suppress their agony. Xuxa followed the map from memory, hoping to reach the suburban enclave a few miles down the road. The air she sucked in through her nose and blew out her mouth burned her lungs, throat, and nostrils. *Something is in the air. An untreated chemical spill?* Her head spun. A haze formed in front of her that her eyes had to fight through. Zombies kept rising, reaching out to her for a violent embrace. In her dazed running, Xuxa tripped over one of the many holes that littered her path. *Is this all on purpose? Who is doing th—* A zombie had grabbed her ankle. Xuxa pulled out her retractable baton, extended it with a flick of her wrist, and bashed the zombie's head in with a flurry of swipes. The sound of dry leaves crunched underfoot. Xuxa rubbed her eyes and saw that the zombie was tied to a slab of buried concrete with a chain. *What is going on?* And then she heard it.

A car raced down the road toward Xuxa, headlights brighter than the sun. They saw her. She knew by the echoing cracks of gunfire piercing the earth around her. Xuxa brought up her Escupeta and fired at the vehicle, knocking out a headlight.

"She's armed! Flank her!"

Are they missing on purpose? Xuxa crouched and headed into the thick forest. There was so much gunfire and breaking shrubbery that Xuxa could barely hear men shouting orders, like ghosts speaking from another plane. She stumbled and couldn't move. A zombie held her in its arms, staring into her eyes, looking for something, mouth babbling like a baby. Xuxa looked back. The zombie's eyes were fogged with pure whiteness. *Is this what everyone sees before they die?* The zombie's head exploded, a rosebud blooming into gore.

"On your fucking knees, now!"

A wall of flashlights shone in Xuxa's eyes, and Xuxa herself was unsure if she'd gone blind from looking into the ghoul's eyes for too long. She did as they said, crumbling to her knees.

"Hands behind your head!"

Xuxa did this, too. She felt someone approaching her, their energy harsh and angry. They put a bag over her head, Xuxa only seeing night. *Or is this what you see before death?*

"Is it one of ours?"

"I don't think so, sir."

"Take her alive! Can't afford to lose another right now."

Then, Xuxa couldn't think anymore.

◎

Zombies raze the settlement. Xuxa is left alone in a small room by her mother who wears her long, black hair in a single braid, who leaves to do her part to fight them off. Xuxa can hear everything: the shooting, screams, the crying, the moans of the undead. She waits until there aren't any more loud sounds, for what seems like hours, just the crackling of fire and low moans. Xuxa's mother hasn't returned. Xuxa is scared. She steps outside, and everything is in ruins: Mrs. Johnson's home burning, the community garden trampled, Dr. López dragging himself to nowhere in particular.

Xuxa can't move. Dr. López sees her and starts to claw his way to her. Xuxa still can't move. He is almost to her feet, wanting to devour Xuxa. Right before Dr. López can reach her legs, a man reveals himself from the ether, taking off his hood, which is slathered in dead meat, the rest of his body covered in dry leaves and hay. He steps on Dr. López's head hard enough to crush it. Xuxa looks at the man. His eyes are calm, and he does not smile.

"Come, child, I will teach you to be invisible."

"What happened?"

"Justice, my child."

"Where's my mom?"

"That's two questions, babosa. There isn't any time for questions anymore."

"Help me."

"I will not help you. I will empower you to do all this," Mil Fuegos says.

◎

Xuxa came to, still only able to see darkness.

"She's awake," one voice said.

Another voice ordered, "Take her to my General."

"Yes, sir."

Sets of arms forced Xuxa to her feet, dragged her through opening and closing doors, outside and inside buildings, until they stopped. The arms placed Xuxa into a chair.

"You can take the bag off now, soldier."

"Yes, my General."

The bag came off, and Xuxa saw an older white man in an ornate military uniform, littered with medals and ribbons of varying colors and sizes, all shiny and bright, sitting behind a big oak desk, polished to perfection. The General inspected her, looked her up and down, never blinked. He opened his mouth to speak.

"You're already dead. We can do with you what we want. At this point, you're living on borrowed time. Listen carefully and consider what I am going to say to you. It's that or I have you killed now."

Xuxa looked back into his eyes, unafraid. Xuxa nodded once.

"Good. We looked through your things. Found these notes," he said, throwing her notebook in front of her. "What are they for?"

"Journaling."

"Cute." The General snapped his fingers. Two guards came over. One restrained her while the other took her right arm and placed it on the desk. A soldier grabbed her pinky and pulled it back far enough to strain her skin. Xuxa moaned but refused to scream. "I think you know what's going to happen next unless you give me real answers," he said, looked directly into her brown eyes.

"I take notes on other communities I encounter," Xuxa responded, breathing in deeper through her nostrils.

"What for?"

"Whether I want to stay or not."

"Smart. Well, the way I see it, you've found the best one. This stronghold was established by me, the most stable, powerful, and growing settlement in the world. We're reestablishing a new world order. A white one, as originally intended until history was routed in the wrong direction. God made the world into shit on seeing how we strayed further and further away from His vision. You see, it's up to me to set history back on track for whites, for humans. God gave us a clean white slate, and we need to keep it that way. As far as I can tell, your kind are no different than those fuck-brains out there."

"What do you want from me?"

The General then lightened up. He leaned back in his chair and put his boots on the desk. "That's what I want to hear. Haw-blahs ess-pan-ole, right? It's in your notes. See, normally, when my men capture a spic like you, they either cave your head in and feed the dogs with your body or assign you labor to do until you fucking die from it and then post you up outside like all the other fuck-brains. Come-pren-day?"

Xuxa nodded.

"I need to hear a 'yes, sir,'" the General said. The soldier that held her finger stretched it farther back, almost to a breaking point.

"Yes, sir," Xuxa choked out.

"Good. Part of this new world for us is that we need a history of the world before all this shit happened. The right history. You see, when we settled this area, we found a library nearby. Thing is, all the books we found were in all kinds of different languages. The last people here must've taken the books in English with them or whatever, but can you see my dilemma? None of us here speak that spic language. Don't need it for the new world we're building. How can you build a glorious future when you don't have the history to back it up? I could make it all up, but there's no need to. Whites built the civilization that held us for centuries before mongrels like you tore it all down. But I figured God was testing me. I was right because here you are. God brought you to my feet to decode the books for me. That's what you're going to do. Translate the books into English, specifically the history books. They'll be brought to me for editing. Then that history will be the foundation that we base this new world upon."

He's a goddamn madman.

"Anyways," the General continued, "you can't escape. You saw how well we've got the surrounding area locked down. If you try to stall our plan with any shenanigans, we'll fuck you up. Understand?"

"Yes, sir," Xuxa said. *I need to buy some time for Mil Fuegos to come at least. He'll ruin this place. Carajo, one tyrant for another.* The soldiers released Xuxa.

"Good. Set her up immediately. Paper, pens. No one fucks with her, is that clear? We need these books translated yesterday," the General said.

"Right away, my General."

"Don't feel bad, sweetheart," the General said, looking again into Xuxa's eyes. He reached into his desk and pulled out Xuxa's bottle of tequila and served two shots: one for himself, one for Xuxa. He waved his soldiers off of Xuxa. "Haven't had tequila since I was a young man, I tell you. Consider it an honor that you're helping the white world begin anew."

Xuxa knocked the shot back, never breaking eye contact with the General.

◎

Mil Fuegos rubs a stick into a tuft of dry grass, small strands of smoke rising.

"Mi nena, escucha," he says. "History has reached its ending point. There is no need to continue humanidad. According to los Aztecas, this is the fifth incarnation of reality. The previous four realities ended in horror: one with jaguars devouring every human, one with a mighty hurricane swallowing every person, one with fire raining down to consume all it touched, one with torrents of blood drowning the earth. The gods, in all their genius, ended our reality with the dead returning to feast upon the living, our collective history catching up to confront us. You see, Xuxa, we were placed in this reality to carry out the will of the gods. That is why we leave nothing left. If it can be destroyed, we fulfill its fate. ¿Entiendes?"

"Sí," Xuxa says.

They are both covered in dirt, blood, grass, and hay to mask themselves from the zombies who are devouring the bodies around them. One tears into the torso of a person like a generous gift, pulling out organs to stuff into their mouth. Other zombies converge upon the same body, fighting each other for flesh. Another zombie sits like a child, licking their fingers to soak up all the blood. Another zombie, all teeth missing, gobs on a sticky mass of crimson gore.

"Never feel bad for destroying a community. If it were meant to last, the gods would not have let us find them, mi nena."

Xuxa looks into his eyes. Mil Fuegos's fire starts.

◎

Xuxa sat in a classroom with four large tables, seats, a stack of blank paper, a cup filled with many different types of pens, and in a corner, a pile of books that reached her knees. She'd never had access to so many books at once. Mil Fuegos had taught her how to read in English and Spanish but only let her choose from a specially curated list of texts that included religious materials, medical books, and weapons manuals. Whenever they encountered a library, Mil Fuegos set fire to it faster than anything else, the black smoke of burning ink staining the blue sky. A feeling of excitement overwhelmed her as she saw so many different covers for different stories by different people, even though the guard kept her hand-cuffs tight on her wrists albeit with a longer chain. Many books were in Spanish, but some were in languages she didn't recognize; some used lines and circles, some looked similar to English and Spanish, even using the same alphabet, but the words were nothing she recognized. *How deep the world was before all this happened.* "Hey, hurry up. Find a history book and get to work," her assigned guard said. A white woman, she had on desert camouflage pants, a beige shirt and hat, sunglasses, blond hair in a ponytail, black gloves, a belt with a walkie talkie, and a spare magazine for her AR-15 that she held at the ready. *At least I can read and learn some things before Mil Fuegos arrives. It's just a matter of waiting.*

Xuxa picked up a few books, carrying as many possible in her arms like a load of gold and took them to a table. She read the titles of the books before her: *El manual de árboles locales, Ciencia de la tierra: octava edición, Las escrituras de Gabriel García Márquez, Enciclopedia mundial 1996: TUV, Atlas mundial 1983, Diccionario español, Obras completas de Frida Kahlo,* and *La historia de los estados unidos: 1751–1900.* The Frida Kahlo book held gorgeous images of a woman who was a stag, portraits, and surreal paintings of pain. Xuxa nearly cried from their beauty. She then looked through the others, reading their tables of contents, their first and last sentences. The Márquez one had several interesting titles in it. It began with a book: "Muchos años después, frente al pelotón de fusilamiento . . ." It ended with a speech: "Una nueva y arrasadora utopía de la vida, donde nadie pueda decidir por otros hasta la forma de morir . . ."

Everything else seemed straightforward by their titles: The encyclopedias had short information blurbs about a topic, but only for the certain parts of the alphabet that the book held. The earth sciences book had a periodic table and an index. The atlas had large, colorful maps of places all over the world. The tree manual listed trees like acacia, cypress, and yaupon. However, Xuxa kept running into a word she didn't recognize. *What the hell is "Texas?"* Xuxa had

"I need some of the other books to look words up," Xuxa said.

"Fine. Let's see, this one doesn't seem to be of any use to us," the guard said, picking up the Frida Kahlo book. She then threw the book to the ground and fired rounds into it, shredding the pages into slivers of colors. Xuxa's ears rang while she hid the Márquez book under another. *What you love most they will kill first.* The guard's walkie-talkie spoke.

"Shots fired. What was that?"

"It was me, just teaching the spic a lesson," the guard responded into the machine. Xuxa still didn't understand what that word meant, *spic*, but they kept calling her that.

"Be careful. My General was very clear on not hurting her too bad."

"Yes, sir." The guard put away her walkie talkie. "You, get to fucking work before my General gets bored with you."

Xuxa complied. She translated as much of the American history book as she could, discovering new, horrible things about the world before: slavery, racism, civil war, genocide, assassinations, etc. *Nations were built to empower one set of people, then disempower others. Are we doomed to repeat all this?*

At the end of the day, the guard looked at all the writing Xuxa had done and took all the pages, placed them in a folder, and asked Xuxa to step over the chain of the handcuffs so that her hands were behind her back. Xuxa was escorted to her cell, but not before witnessing the society the General had built. In a way, it was perfect, the suburban homes painted with fresh coats of white paint, green grass, clean streets, denizens walking around unworried and with clean clothes. In the distance, she saw a well-constructed wall. Xuxa couldn't see anyone who looked like herself, however, everyone pale-skinned. *Of course. Just like in the books.* There were even crops in the far corner with nonwhite people working the dirt and guards with guns patrolling it.

The guard took Xuxa to a wall (one that wasn't as large as the outer wall) where there was a small opening, filled with guards and weapons, something that the area she had just walked through lacked. Barbed wire lined the top of this smaller wall, and guards were stationed at intervals along it. Another guard confronted Xuxa and her escort.

"Oh, is this the special spic?" the other guard laughed. He grabbed Xuxa by the chin and shook her head. Xuxa put her body's weight on her left leg, then kicked with all her strength with her right leg. She drove her foot into the belly of the guard and sent him flying back. Guns turned on Xuxa.

"Don't shoot! My General gave very specific orders to not shoot this one!"

The guns lowered. The kicked guard rose to his feet and slapped Xuxa.

"Bitch! Get her the fuck out of my sight!"

Xuxa, bleeding from the mouth, was then shoved past the wall where a woman waited for her. She wore a shawl, had bright brown eyes, and was darker-skinned than Xuxa. The guard took off Xuxa's handcuffs and pushed her toward the other woman.

"She is to report to this station tomorrow morning at dawn. You understand?"

"Yes, ma'am."

"She's even a minute late, you're fucking dead."

"Yes, ma'am," the woman responded. The wall door was closed behind them. "Come on. I'm supposed to show you where you sleep."

"Who are you?"

"I'm Tierra, your escort."

"Tierra? Like Earth?"

"Ha. Yes. Like Earth. You are Xuxa, correct? You kicking that guard was hilarious. I like you already. But you need to cut that shit out from here on out. I'm now liable for your actions."

Xuxa saw the community before her. It was squalid. The homes made of spare wood and sheet metal. No grass grew, just dirt and dust. *It looks like the bastards just tore down the homes here. Why? Out of spite?* Then Xuxa saw that the denizens looked more like herself, darker-skinned than those on the other side of the wall, brown and black and varying shades of both. There were no children or older people. On one of the walls, bodies hung from nooses, knives stuck in their bodies with signs reading, "Can't escape," "Don't try," "Failure." Xuxa looked but didn't say anything. *I can see why Mil Fuegos wants what he wants.*

"Just ignore that. Those are people who tried to escape, but I heard it's awful out there. Got the place rigged to make it impossible to make it far."

"Yeah, I know." Xuxa remembered the blurring of her senses, the zombies chained to their stations. "Is this how the General has all of you living? Whites on one side, not white on this side?"

"Yes."

"I've read this in the history books . . ."

"History repeats itself, yes. I know."

"How do you . . ."

"I used to be a history teacher, before all this."

"How old are you?"

"That's rude. Come on already, let me take you to your space and get you some food. We can talk more then."

Along the way, Xuxa saw people lying on the floor from hunger and exhaustion. But she also saw people crafting furniture, singing, playing games she didn't understand. *The General is simply recreating history. I cannot let him. What knowledge is worth learning that is based on the suffering of others? Is it truly knowledge if it is not accessible to others? This nightmare stops here. I'm starting to sound more like Mil Fuegos . . .*

Tierra led Xuxa to a small hut with a single candle burning, a yellow glow in the darkness. Xuxa sat on the floor in front of a small table while Tierra served herself and Xuxa corn mush and water.

"I'm sharing some of my rations with you, so you enjoy every bite and sip of that for me," Tierra said before raising a cup to her lips.

"Thank you. What does spic mean?" Xuxa asked. Tierra choked on her water.

"Is that what they've been calling you? Damn. It's all right, they call me worse."

"I assumed it was bad. But what is it?"

"Let's just say it's not a nice word for people who look like you. A very bad word."

"Of course. Listen, Tierra, we've got to get out of here. Fast."

"Go figure. You listen, Xuxa. We've tried that. We've tried to escape, but things only get worse from there. You saw. We all love each other here too much to make it worse for others. Understand? If you try anything, they'll hurt us. You are part of something bigger now, so try and get used to that."

Xuxa wasn't used to this, her actions accountable to others. *Is this what a community is like?* Xuxa told Tierra everything: her orders from the General, what she read, Mil Fuegos's colossal army of the undead, and how close he was, perhaps only a day away.

"Holy shit. How do you know this person?"

"He raised me, taught me everything I know. Now I wander. His name, it means . . ."

"One thousand fires," Tierra said.

"You speak Spanish?"

"Sí."

"But the General said that I was the only person to speak Spanish he knows."

"The General is a piece of shit, but he isn't dumb. He killed everyone he caught speaking it. Some of us stopped because of that. He said that to you so you wouldn't know anything. Now that he's found all these books, he needs Spanish speakers. He's going to kill you after you translate the books, you know. In fact, he's probably going to kill me too after spending time with you."

"So you'll help me? When Mil Fuegos's army arrives, we need to blow open a hole in the wall to make sure we get out of here. You and everyone can escape through the opening as the soldiers deal with the undead."

"Blow open a hole in the wall? What the hell are you talking about?"

"An explosive. We can make one and blow a fucking hole in the wall. It's not too big of a wall, but it could be enough to stall Mil Fuegos. We weaken their defenses, and that way we can be sure this place is fucked."

"How do we make an explosive?"

"I saw they have green grass and crops on the other side. That means you use fertilizer, right? They also have cars, which means gasoline, sí? Mix them and boom." Xuxa recalled all the times Mil Fuegos taught her to make explosives of various kinds using different chemicals and detonators. *Imagínate que estás mezclando masa para pastelito*, he once said, pouring gasoline into a ditch of fertilizer to blow open a safe.

"Yeah, but how do we get the mixture right?"

"I've got that part down." Xuxa wrote down the ingredients for a fertilizer-based explosive on a piece of paper with a pen she had taken from the room.

"It's gonna take a minute to make this. We have our own resistance going on, so I'm going to have to convince the others."

"We have a day. I just need help getting the supplies and setting them up. That's it. You can leave as soon as the fuse is lit," Xuxa assured.

"Alright. We're not losing anyone for you or whatever this is, though. Supplies and a blast. That's it, and we're out. Get some sleep. I'll get this out to the right people."

"The guards will be focused on Mil Fuegos's army, so I wouldn't worry too much about fighting. But you may have to procure your own weapons for the outside."

"We'll see."

◎

In the darkness of a night, Mil Fuegos shoots an arrow from his bow into a person serving as a lookout on their community's wall, who collapses like a song note. He then asks for his next arrow. Xuxa hands him one wrapped in rag wet with gasoline and a match. Mil Fuegos lights it, loads it into his bow, and releases it into the wall. Mil Fuegos runs and Xuxa follows. The vanguard of his undead army staggers to the wall in minutes, attracted by the light, banging on it, causing it to waver. Xuxa can hear the clamoring of people, shouting to get organized and mount a defense. But it's too late.

Xuxa hands over fireworks to Mil Fuegos, who lights and fires them into the air, an artificial constellation for his army of zombies to follow. Their moans echo throughout the night like ocean waves pulled by the moon's glow. Mil Fuegos unravels the rope around his waist and ties a grappling hook to it, throwing it over another section of the wall. He and Xuxa climb it to the top. Everyone is distracted by the horde smashing through the front gates, so Mil Fuegos and Xuxa assemble Molotov cocktails to throw at homes and people—oil rags stuffed in bottles of gasoline, ends lit, then thrown. There's so much light in this world, Xuxa thinks.

Someone sees them, points at them. Mil Fuegos promptly fires an arrow into his heart. Finally, Mil Fuegos fires an arrow with dynamite at the gate. It explodes. The zombies enter in gushes like blood pooling around a deep wound. Mil Fuegos and Xuxa fire arrows at the legs of fleeing people, forcing them to fall and cry at their impending doom. They are immediately devoured. Some zombies tear first at their bellies and pull out gobs of organs. Others bite off fingers from hands. Others ravage the faces as their mouths scream until they can scream no longer. Mil Fuegos gasps at the beauty of his phantasmagoria, nose pointed upward toward the sky and nostrils expanding to profoundly take it all in. Xuxa watches neither in pleasure nor horror. It takes an hour.

Mil Fuegos and Xuxa begin a sweep and find cans of food. They sit down to eat as the flames and zombies continue their work. With a spoonful of beans near his mouth, Mil Fuegos notices a family trying to escape. He points at them with his spoon.

"Termínalos, Xuxa." Xuxa nods and follows them.

*She catches up to them and fires an arrow into the back of the patri-
arch, who falls like a tree. The mother and daughter turn and weep,
begging Xuxa for mercy. Xuxa looks at them. She doesn't want to do
this, their cries pulling the tears from her own eyes.*

*"Ya sabía," Mil Fuegos says, walking in from behind Xuxa. "You are
going to have to get used to this, Xuxa. Remember, the gods would not
have put them in our path if they didn't deserve this fate." He pulls out
his club. The mother and daughter put their hands up in vain.*

*The mother and daughter look at Xuxa and scream her name as Mil
Fuegos walks at them, raising his club in the air.*

Xuxa. Xuxa!

◎

Xuxa woke up covered in sweat. Tierra was snapping her fingers and
calling her name to awaken her. Tierra's eyes were bloodshot, and
bags hung under them as though she hadn't slept all night.

"We're getting everything together."

"Ok. Muy bien," Xuxa said, still rusty from her sleep.

"Hurry and get up before you get me killed."

At the checkpoint, the guards put Xuxa in handcuffs and handed
her off to a different guard than before.

"Special orders from my General. I'm to take her directly to him."

Handed off and escorted through the main area of the settlement, Xuxa memorized the way to where the General stayed. When
they arrived, the guard knocked on a large door.

"Come in!" the General shouted. The guard opened the door and
shoved Xuxa in, closing the door behind her. "Have a seat. I saw
your translations from yesterday. Very direct. That's good. I've got
some notes for you. Watch."

The General pulled out the same folder from yesterday and
took out the papers within it. He began showing Xuxa his editing
process. For example, the paragraph about Texas history that Xuxa
translated earlier now read:

Texas was the greatest state in the United States. Mexico tyranni-
cally controlled the territory through oppressive laws that robbed
Texans of their rights until 1836 when Texas fought and unilat-
erally won its independence. The U.S. annexed Texas, and they
both triumphantly defeated Mexico in a war in 1846. A slave nation
under God, the U.S. and Texas enjoyed prosperity and entered a
long period of economic growth.

The General made other sweeping changes. The preamble to the
Constitution now read:

We the White People of the United States, in order to form a more
perfect Union, establish Justice, ensure domestic Tranquility, pro-
vide for the common defense, promote the general Welfare of
Whiteness, uphold a Christian God, and secure the Blessings of
Liberty to Whites and their Posterity, do ordain and establish this
Constitution for the United States of America.

Xuxa could have laughed at all this if it wasn't so real. *Who's to say
it wasn't really like this? What good is this history other than to avoid
it? People like him only wish to hear the history they've written. What
does he even need me for?*
"You see what I want? I want you to do all this because it's
important that your kind accept this history the most. That this is
how it's always been, and how it will always be. Got it?"
"Yes, sir."
"Good. Get back to work," the General said. However, his walkie-
talkie garbled, then said in clear words:
"My General, permission to report."
"Go on."
"We've found something odd. One of the undead has been found
with something strange."
"Oh yeah? Spit it out."
"It seems to have purposely been slathered with red paint."

"What? Why the hell do I care?"

"Sir, this is the second one we've found this month."

I killed the third one. He's coming! I have to let Tierra know.

"Just keep your wits about you. You think the undead have formed their own country or something? Don't waste my time."

"Yes, my General."

"General, may I say something?" Xuxa asked.

"What the fuck do you want?"

"I can get this process done faster. I just need an assistant to help me look through the books. They just need to know the word *historia* and separate the books that have that from the others. That's all. Just give me Tierra since she knows me already."

"Fine. Just get to work. Everyone is being a pain in my ass today. Lucky I got this." The General pulled out Xuxa's bottle of tequila from his desk and waved it to mock her.

You will die soon enough, pendejo.

In the room full of books and blank paper, Xuxa, hands laid on the table before her in handcuffs, waited for Tierra's arrival. *Oh fuck, he's coming, he's coming, he's coming. We'll have to mix and detonate on-site for this to work fast enough. Let's hope her people can get the stuff quickly in time.* There was a knock on the door.

A guard brought in Tierra blindfolded and in handcuffs at the end of a rifle. Tierra looked angry. The guard removed the blindfold and handcuffs slowly, methodically. Tierra walked over calmly.

"Yes, ma'am? How can I help you?" she said, as though she didn't know Xuxa. The guard pulled up a chair at the front of the room and sat, AR-15 resting in her lap.

Through clenched teeth, Xuxa responded, "Sit down, please," setting a chair next to herself.

"What the fuck is going on?" Tierra asked.

"He's coming tonight!" Xuxa said.

"¿Pues, qué chingado vamos a hacer aquí?" Tierra whispered through her teeth.

"Hey, what's with all the whispering?" the guard piped in.

"Tenemos que hacer algo inmediatamente," Xuxa stressed.

"Necesitamos más tiempo. Tenemos gente juntando los materiales."

"I'm coming over there!" the guard shouted, AR-15 at her shoulder.

"Nothing, nothing!" Tierra yelled back, hands up, palms facing the guard. Xuxa sat silently.

The guard shouted commands to Tierra, "On your knees! Hands behind your head! Now!" Xuxa noticed it was the white woman from yesterday. Tierra followed the commands, staring at Xuxa with wide eyes to compel her to do something. "You, spic! What is going on?" Her rifle was situated at the back of Tierra's head.

Xuxa weakly pointed to the stack of books in the far corner. The guard turned her head to see. "The—the book. It—It's—"

Tierra turned around, grabbed the end of the rifle, and pushed away from herself. Xuxa stood and punched the guard in the throat. The rifle fired three rounds into a corner. Tierra wrestled the AR-15 from the guard's hands while Xuxa wrapped her handcuff chain around the neck of the guard, fell backward, and pulled tight, her knees in the guard's back. Xuxa pulled and pulled. The guard choked, spat blood, and tried to loosen the grip of the chain with her fingers, legs flailed like the tail of a breathless fish. Tierra pointed the rifle at the guard but let Xuxa finish. Xuxa pulled until the flailing weakened, spasmed, then stopped, before she let go. Xuxa lifted her arms and kicked the guard off herself, spitting at her body immediately afterward. The radio talked.

"Shots fired. What's going on in there?"

"What the fuck was that? I had a plan!" Xuxa asked as she caught her breath.

"I had to do something! I had no other choice! The bitch was gonna shoot me to teach your dumbass a lesson!"

"Give me the walkie-talkie!" Tierra wrangled the walkie-talkie from the dead guard's belt and threw it to Xuxa.

"I repeat, shots fired. Is everything okay?" the radio asked. Xuxa breathed in deeply and did her best imitation of the guard, rubbing the speaker of the walkie-talkie. "Had to teach the spic another lesson."

"Ok. Be sure to turn in your talkie for repair."

"Yes, sir."

The radio stopped speaking.

Xuxa and Tierra looked at each other, surprised they had fooled the soldiers.

Tierra broke the silence. "What now?"

"How long until we get the gas and fertilizer? We'll have to mix and detonate on-site. It'll have to be quick. If I'm lucky, it should work."

"I don't know! You said we had twenty-four hours!"

"I said we had a day! Never mind. We'll have to wait until Mil Fuegos makes his move. The guards will be occupied."

"Are you sure?"

"We don't have any other option. We'll have to sit by the radio and listen and move fast." Xuxa searched the guard's body and found a pistol, a spare magazine for the AR-15, and the keys for her handcuffs, which Tierra removed. Tierra handed the rifle over, but Xuxa insisted Tierra take the pistol. They both sat and waited.

"I can't believe it. This is going to end," Tierra laughed, almost crying.

"I hope so."

"No. It must end, Xuxa. It must," Tierra pleaded, looking deeply into Xuxa's eyes.

Xuxa picked up a book and weighed it in her hands. "Did you know that some people die making sure certain ideas don't take hold, Tierra?"

"Yes. I know."

"I promise you, nothing of that madman's ideas will leave here tonight. Even if I have to die," Xuxa said. She looked at the book in her hand and saw it was the Márquez book, the one she made sure to hide. *Una nueva y arrasadora utopía de la vida, donde nadie pueda decidir por otros hasta la forma de morir* . . . Xuxa ripped the book in half down the spine since it was so big and secured both halves in her waistband to take with her. They waited and listened for hours. The radio shouted.

"Alert! An arrow has been shot at the main gate. It seems to be on fire. Investigating."

"There he is," Xuxa said. She rose to her feet and readied her rifle.

When they left the building, Xuxa heard the familiar moans of Mil Fuegos's army. Xuxa and Tierra hid and watched as soldiers ran to the front gate, rounds firing. *There's no coordination among the volleys. Mil Fuegos has only sent his vanguard. We have little time to spare.* "Let's go," Xuxa said.

They ran to the inner wall that separated the white section from the nonwhite section. Xuxa aimed, fired, and killed the guards keeping the laborers in, firing in a cadence so that each shot rang like a tolling bell.

Tierra opened the wall's door, entered, and everyone gathered around her.

"We need the gas and fertilizer now!"

"This way!" someone yelled. *Everyone seems to know what's going on. Is this what a good community is? But really, how many of those can there be left?*

The community led Xuxa and Tierra to the fertilizer and gas. *It still needs to be mixed.* Fireworks exploded in the night sky. *The next wave has begun!* The night moans deepened. Xuxa felt her breath get heavier.

"Let's take this to the back wall before Mil Fuegos gets his army back there!" Xuxa yelled. They all ran together. *Am I part of something?*

Xuxa didn't waste any time as she mixed the gas and fertilizer in the exact proportions Mil Fuegos showed her. *Masa para pastelito* . . . She then instructed everyone to stand far back, far, far back, pouring a trail of gasoline behind herself to light like a detonator.

"Everyone, get down!" Xuxa screamed as she lit the gas trail, flaring in a line, a shining path.

The explosion was grand. Luck favored Xuxa indeed. The air was sucked out of everyone's lungs. They recovered to see a hole in the wall, out into the black night.

"Come on, let's get out of here," Tierra said, grabbing Xuxa by the arm. Xuxa yanked herself from her grasp.

"You have to go, Tierra. Go as far away as you can. Forget this place," Xuxa pleaded. "I have to go back and make sure the General is dead. I promised." Tierra didn't waste time trying to change Xuxa's mind. She only looked into Xuxa's eyes for a single moment, long enough for the two of them to know what it meant: *Good luck.* She handed Xuxa the pistol and said, "I think you'll need this more than me." Tierra then turned around and headed out, the last time Xuxa would see her. *Start something new, something better.*

Xuxa picked up the last of the gas and fertilizer. She held the rifle in her right hand and her eyes looked forward. Xuxa ran toward the white section of the settlement, ready to blow it to hell. Her body shook with fatigue. Soldiers held the line near the front gate, firing in more coordinated efforts. They used the front gate as a funnel to control the flow of Mil Fuegos's army. Xuxa saw the outer wall shaking. *It normally doesn't take this long for Mil Fuegos's army to break through.*

Xuxa stationed herself at the bottom of the shaking wall. *What comes up must come down.* She mixed the ingredients again, pouring them as though laying out a snake's large corpse. *Here I am, doing Mil Fuegos's dirty work. At what point do I get to make my own path?* Xuxa didn't have the gasoline to make a trail long enough to light it from a safe distance. *I have to—* Xuxa looked around, then up. There he was. Mil Fuegos looked down upon her from atop the wall, staring through her. He wore the head of a stag, the horns piercing upward toward the night sky, and a bulletproof vest, his face shrouded in a damp rag. Mil Fuegos picked up his bow and pulled an arrow from his quiver in a seamless motion. Xuxa ran as quickly as possible, for she knew what followed. She could see him in her mind's eye lighting the arrow on fire with an oil rag and match, aiming at the mixture, pulling the arrow back, and letting go. *Boom.* Xuxa fell forward and let the remnants of the smaller blast wash over her body, her lungs unable to take in air.

Xuxa took a moment to breathe. Her torso muscles ached from expansion, and she rolled onto her back. Xuxa looked into the sky, coughing and sucking in as much air as her mouth could swallow. Mil Fuegos was gone. *Back to his chaos.* Zombies piled in through the new hole, hungry and desperate. A zombie approached Xuxa, but she mustered enough strength to kick it over, following that up with an elbow to its skull. She rose to her feet and ran. Soldiers began firing at her. Xuxa noticed that she had dropped her rifle in her sprint, only having a pistol. *This is more than enough to kill that pendejo.* Xuxa ran for cover. The shooting accelerated, and she saw that the zombies overran the soldiers from two sides now.

She lugged her body to the General's office, as though drunk. *He's likely gone by now. Maybe I can recover something useful from his office. Everything hurts.*

She approached the big door but didn't knock. He was there, sitting at his desk, drinking Xuxa's tequila.

"You're here," Xuxa said, surprised. "You know, other men like yourself try to make a run for it."

"Only defeated men run," he said, sniffing the tequila's aroma from the top of his glass. "You're a fool if you think 1 was the only one. A nation like this isn't simply alone. 1 exist because it works, because there's so many of us." The General leaned his head back to swallow the tequila shot. Xuxa shot him in the heart immediately. *Then it'll be my life's mission to kill the rest of your kind.*

She retrieved her bottle, now with only half left, and took a swig. She searched his desk. The folder was there. Xuxa held the translated pages and dropped them outside a window. Some floated away into the ether. Other pages fell into flames, the burning edges crinkling like the fingers of a dying man.

Xuxa searched her surroundings. Every building in the settlement burned. Homes collapsed under the heat. Zombies devoured the bodies with large chomps and deep swallows. This was the highest number of undead Xuxa had seen. No one alive. Except for Mil Fuegos, who sat nearby with a stack of books, knees almost to his chest, reading one that seemed to have engrossed him as he rubbed his chin. He looked up, as though he felt Xuxa's eyes on him. He smiled and waved.

"I saw you blow that wall open! Just like I taught you! Don't you miss this, Xuxa?" he yelled. He jumped to his feet and spun in a circle, arms spread open like a dervish.

Xuxa stepped back, pistol at the ready. *He's coming.* Mil Fuegos leapt like the stag he wore, making his way into the General's office. Xuxa kept her pistol aimed at his face.

"¿Qué haces aquí? Are you following me, nena?"

"I'm going to kill you."

"Ha. Going around thinking there's still something to be saved," Mil Fuegos said, "Why, you must be the last real person alive, eh? Créeme, Xuxa, eres La Última que cree en este mundo. Hope died long ago, before any of this."

Xuxa squeezed the trigger. Mil Fuegos moved in time to dodge the bullet and wrestled the gun from her hand, pushing her backward. He aimed the pistol at her, hesitated to shoot.

"You saw what this place was. You'll join me again, soon enough. You simply aren't ready," he said, as though placing a curse. Mil Fuegos kept the pistol drawn at Xuxa as he backed up toward the window he leapt in from. He fell backwards, laughing.

There's the General's model for the world, then there's Mil Fuegos's. Men only live for the past. How do we begin the world anew for everyone? I don't know. I don't know. I don't know.

Xuxa escaped the settlement, witnessing once more the zombies devouring bodies, the wet chewing of organs and wet sucking of bone, and quietly piercing the skulls of any that approached her with a knife. Xuxa walked and walked, book in her belt. She picked up a shotgun off of a dead soldier along the way, her new Escupeta, but didn't fire it out of fear of attracting the undead. She escaped the settlement and slowly made her way up a hill. Xuxa looked backward at the horizon, lit with a roaring fire. Tears leaked from Xuxa's eyes. She tasted salt.

I'll be ready for you one day, Mil Fuegos.

◎

Xuxa, La Última, approaches the tired guard holding the old rifle standing atop the makeshift wall. The old rifle points in her direction, slightly shaking, the barrel moving like a bird's eye.

"Who—who are you?"

"Porfa, my name is Alondra, and I'm tired of wandering," Xuxa says, laying down La Escupeta and machete at her feet. "None of the undead are too close by. I escaped them about three miles back." The guard lowers their rifle and calls out to others, now stepping down to disappear behind the wall. The makeshift wall clumsily opens, the bottom scraping along the dirt. A woman with long black hair, dressed in dirty jeans and a brown shirt runs out with a bottle of water.

She asks, out of breath, "Are you all right? How long have you been out there? Please come in." Her voice reminds Xuxa of Tierra, whom she hasn't seen since that collapsing night years ago.

Why are they so welcoming? Perhaps they are naïve. Perhaps they've been wanderers, too. Whatever the reason, Xuxa, La Última, has hope.

ABOUT THE AUTHOR

Reyes Ramirez is a Houstonian, writer, educator, curator, and organizer of Mexican and Salvadoran descent. Reyes won the 2019 YES Contemporary Art Writer's Grant, 2017 Blue Mesa Review Nonfiction Contest, and 2014 riverSedge Poetry Prize and has poems, stories, essays, and reviews in *Indiana Review, Cosmonauts Avenue, Queen Mob's Teahouse, Speculative Fiction for Dreamers: A Latinx Anthology, december magazine, Arteinformado, Texas Review, Houston Noir, Gulf Coast Journal, The Acentos Review, Cimarron Review,* and elsewhere. He is a 2020 CantoMundo Fellow, 2021 Interchange Artist Grant Fellow, 2022 Crosstown Arts Writer in Residence, and has been awarded grants from the Houston Arts Alliance, Poets & Writers, and The Warhol Foundation's Idea Fund. Read more of his work at reyesvramirez.com.